CARTEL

ARIES MANIFESTO

QUEEN

A CARTEL NOVEL

JAQUAVIS

NY TIMES BEST SELLING AUTHOR

COLEMAN

"IF YOU LOVE SOMETHING, LET IT GO..."

If you love something... let it go. And if it comes back to you, then it's truly yours. That quote repeatedly played inside Aries' mind. She heard it from a song many moons ago, and it has never genuinely resignated until that moment. The sky was eerily dark, and there weren't any stars out. There was only the full moon, which provided illumination. Aries' eyes were full of tears and she shook her head, trying to get the phrase out. She couldn't because the voice was just too loud within. The cold wind blew as Aries stood on top of the thirty-two story building. She stood at the edge, and the faint sounds of cars driving by were the only thing she heard. Aries finally released a tear. The tears that built in her eyes finally overflowed and dropped. Aries felt knots in the pit of her stomach, a pain she had never felt before. It was the vilest ache that she had ever experienced. She knew exactly what it was... it was the burden of guilt.

Aries looked down at her arms and slowly examined her inner forearms as her eyes gradually climbed to her wrists. Her hands were extended in front of her, hanging over the building. Gradually, she began to hear more than the passing cars and traffic noises from below as her brain registered what she was looking at. A baby's cries were now drowning out any other sounds. The baby was squirming, and the baby's face was beet red from the wailing as Aries held on tightly, firmly gripping the baby's underarms. The tears were pouring from Aries' pupils, and her emotional faucet had been turned on. She was mentally slipping, and her hands shook uncontrollably as she stared at a mirror image of herself.

The eyes, the ears, and the skin tones were identical, adding to the anguish and the weight of the situation. Her lips quivered and the pain was intense; she could feel the uncomfortable knots in the pit of her stomach.

"If you love something..."

Those were the last words before she released the crying baby, letting the infant freefall. Aries immediately looked over the ledge and reached out her arms, instantly regretting what she had just done. As the tears poured down her face, she lifted her shaking hand and covered her mouth. Aries let out a roar unlike she had ever done before. She watched as her newborn cried and flailed her arms, not fully understanding what was happening.

Aries heard a sound coming from the baby; that was weird. The baby was no longer crying, but now the baby was making a strange noise. Aries couldn't understand, and her mind couldn't register the foreign sound. Her baby was making an alarm sound. Aries was confused as she turned her head sideways as the baby continued to fall.

The buzzing of the alarm clock woke Aries out of her horrible nightmare. Knots had formed in her stomach as she grimaced and clutched her midsection. She balled into a fetal position as she sucked air through her clenched teeth, waiting for the unbearable pain to subside. She looked over at the alarm clock, which was still sounding off and only making the matter worse. She reached over and hit the button, instantly silencing it. Aries' eyes focused on the two medicine bottles next to the clock, which both had her name on them. The doctor had prescribed them to her just the day before. One was antibiotics, and the other was painkillers to cope with the aches of aborting a child.

Aries sat up and placed her feet on the warm, wooden floors. She loved how the sun kissed the wood every morning and naturally heated the floors. It had been almost five years since she had relocated to her hometown of Barbados. Her roots were embedded in the small place called Bridgetown. Every day it seemed like she woke up in heaven... every day, except that one. This dreadful morning was the only bad day she had since returning home. And it was a reason for that... his name was Saint.

Saint was the man who fathered her aborted child, and unbeknownst to him, she had found out she was pregnant and immediately scheduled the procedure. Aries' heart was heavy for more than one reason, she had a significant burden to bear. The weight of everything she had gone through over the past year was currently on her shoulders. She gently placed her hand on the back of her neck and slowly rotated her head. Her other hand was still firmly on her stomach; she felt like shit.

"Fuck," she whispered as she realized what the day would bring.

Hard decisions were made, and on that day, she

would have to deal with the mental strain of her choices. She reached over and took the medication, using the glass of water on the nightstand to wash it down. She then stood up and walked to the front balcony connected to her bedroom. She instantly noticed the familiar sounds of the townspeople below as she peeked down.

Bridgetown was a high tourist area, so every day new faces walked up and down the streets. The town's brick road was filled with an abundance of boutique shops. The rear of her brownstone faced the beautiful ocean, so she had the best of both worlds. She saw people standing at the building directly below her brownstone's door, but they would walk away after a few seconds because of a big sign that read "closed today" was on the door.

Aries had a small restaurant that served the island's signature dish, jerk chicken, and various sides. It was one of the more popular spots on the island, but on that day, Aries would have to shut down shop for the obvious. She heard chatter coming from her home. She looked towards her bedroom door and instantly recognized the woman's voice. She almost forgot that she had a guest and got herself together to be a good host.

Aries made her way downstairs and entered the

spacious back kitchen area. She then saw her best friend in life, Miamor Jones. Only one month removed from a federal penitentiary, there she was in the flesh. Miamor sat at the small dining table with a designer silk robe on. Her hair was neatly tied into a bun on the top of her head. She was curled up comfortably with a cup of coffee in her hand. She sipped as she watched a young man standing at the sink, scrubbing his hands vigorously over the kitchen sink. Pink suds were on his hands and tattooed forearms as he looked back at Aries.

"Hey, Auntie Aries," the young man said. He had on a black jogging suit and a bandana around his neck.

"Good morning, girl," Miamor said with her signature, beautiful smile.

"Hey CJ," Aries said as she walked towards Miamor and hugged her. "Hey, Mia," she added before making her way over to the sink. She stood in front of her nephew, who was now towering over her. He turned towards her and dried his hands with a nearby towel. Aries smiled and stared at the young man in awe.

"Oh me God. Look at yu'. You look just like yo' damn daddy," Aries said with her heavy Caribbean accent.

CJ childishly smiled and dropped his head. The mention of his deceased father always gave him a bittersweet feeling inside. Aries placed her hands on both cheeks and stared into his eyes. She then pulled him into her warm embrace and closed her eyes. CJ made sure to hug her tight, knowing that she had just lost a child. He could feel her pain.

"Thank you for coming to handle that for me," Aries whispered as she rocked back and forth.

"That's what family is for," he whispered to her.

"Bitch, I didn't get a hug like that. I'm the one that put this together for you," Miamor playfully said as she stood up and smiled. She folded her arms across her chest, displaying her fake attitude. Aries instantly smiled and turned to Miamor.

"Come on. Yu' still don't play about me, me see," Aries said as she put her hands on her hips and cocked her head to the side. She then extended her arms and walked towards Miamor. They embraced and hugged each other tightly. It had been years since they were able to hug one another. They had been through so much in their past life. Although Miamor had just come home, when Aries called her with a problem, she was there. Miamor wasn't even allowed to leave the country because of her parole stipulations, but when she got that call...

***

The smell of burnt breakfast sausage and the fire alarm sounded throughout the air, waking Saint from his peaceful slumber. He instantly sat up and took a deep breath as he wiped the cold from his eyes. He stretched his hands above his head and let out a toe-curling yawn. He quickly went to the French doors that led to the ocean. He smiled and shook his head, knowing that his 'Lovey' had probably gotten too caught up in her morning talk shows and burnt breakfast. Saint rubbed his slightly protruding belly that sat just above his beltline.

Saint wasn't fat by any means, but the extra belly came from years of good eating and living the good life. His shoulders and arm were intact; the stomach in front of him showed his comfortable lifestyle. He smiled as he ran his tongue over his top row of teeth. They were perfect and white... opposite of the bottom row. Pure gold slugs were across his bottom row, giving a rugged look. Although Saint was very articulate, intelligent, and stoic; his gold slugs were a pure indication of what he was. His full, neatly trimmed beard was perfectly symmetrical around his lips, and he had a beautiful smile. Some would call him a monster, but the ones that truly knew him called him a saint. The irony.

"Lovey! You left the stove on again!" Saint yelled as he looked back, so his grandmother could hear him from where he was in the back bedroom. Saint paused and waited for her response. The only thing he heard was the loud sounds of Wendy Williams coming from the television. He smiled and shook his head, knowing that she was hard of hearing and always would blast the television, but she usually waited until he was up before her shenanigans started.

"Alright, Lovey... here I come," Saint said to himself as he smiled and shook his head.

He loved living with his grandma in her home country. It had been her dream to come back to the islands and live out the remainder of her life. So, about a year before, Saint had purchased her an immaculate villa right off the ocean. He relocated her there for good it was something that Saint needed as well. He needed an escape from his former life in the States. He had done many things on the wrong side of the law and was fortunate enough to avoid jail time or, even worse, death. Lovey would thank him every morning for making her dreams come true, but Saint was even more thankful. He loved that he could see his only living relative every single day, and just like old times, she would make him breakfast every morning and made his bed for him at night.

Although Saint was well off and could afford to housekeep, it meant more to him to make his grandmother feel needed. They were two peas in a pod, and Saint was happier than he'd been in a while. His grandmother was his best friend. His quality of life had elevated since they both moved to the island.

Saint quickly ran water over his face and threw on a t-shirt before heading into the kitchen area, which sat in the middle of the luxury villa. Lovey always wanted a spacious kitchen, and Saint ensured she had one. She had more than enough room to cook anytime she wanted. Saint rubbed his stomach and knew that Lovey was part of why he was holding some of that gut.

"What you got burning in here, girl?" Saint playfully said as he walked onto the marble floors that opened to the kitchen area. Saint walked in smiling, and the first thing he saw was smoke coming from the stove area.

"Oh shit," he whispered as he hurried over to the stove.

The smoke detector was still beeping and made things more chaotic. Also, the sound of the television being to the max was distracting. As Saint approached the stove, he quickly turned the burner off. There were six sausage links in the skillet burned to a crisp. He looked over to the stove and saw burnt biscuits inside as well.

"Grandma!" Saint yelled, only using that name when he was in trouble or something was wrong. "Girl, you un' forgot about everything! Almost burned the house down," Saint said while laughing to himself, grabbing the skillet, and placing it over the sink. He turned on the water to cool the skillet, causing a gush of steam to rise into the air. Everything seemed so hectic because of all the noises, not to mention the nerve wrecking alarm. Saint hurried over to the kitchen drawer to grab a dish towel to fan the alarm. Saint felt something wet on the floor, and he quickly raised his foot while looking down. It was a red liquid.

"What the fuck?" Saint whispered as he squinted his eyes.

He then noticed that it was coming from somewhere. His eyes followed the path of the thick maroon color liquid, and everything froze when he saw the source of the blood. It was Lovey. In a matter of a second, time froze. He didn't hear the loudness of the television anymore. He didn't hear the irritating sound of the smoke detector nor the sound of the sizzling skillet from the sausages. The only sense that was working was his sight, he had become entirely numb.

He looked down at her body, which had on a morning gown and a cooking apron. As his eyes slowly traveled up her body, he saw the unthinkable. Her head was gone and severed from her body. . Guts and body pieces he'd never seen before were spilling from her neck, where her head used to be.

"No… no… no, Grandma," Saint said as he dropped to his knees, trying to put the contents spilling out of her neck back into the corpse. He was in shock; his mind didn't know what to do. His hands shook vigorously, and his eyes bucked as he examined her bloody body. Saint's hands fidgeted nervously around what used to be the woman he held closest to his heart. He sat on his knees and felt like he was in the middle of a nightmare. He instantly stood up and looked around. He yelled for Jupe, his personal shooter that always protected his home while he was asleep. He would station himself on the front porch and walk around the house every night.

"Jupe!!! Jupe!!!" Saint yelled as he looked around feverishly, searching for his personal bodyguard. It wasn't until he stepped out of the kitchen and partially into the living room that he saw Jupe. His body was lying there lifeless… also decapitated. Jupe's head was missing from his body. Saint's stomach dropped at the gruesome sight. Saint was stuck.

As he looked closer, he noticed that the eyes of Lovey and Jupe were looking at him. Their two heads were lined up inside Lovey's China cabinet on top of two dish plates. One head on each platter. Their heads were on display as if it was a twisted art exhibit. Saint stiffened and blinked his bloodshot red eyes, not believing what he saw was real. However, it was true. This was his reality. This wasn't a dream by any stretch of the imagination. It was karma…

Chapter One

A MURDER OF CROWS

(ONE YEAR EARLIER)

The night's air was thick and humid as the massive crowd filled the large hut. A neon-colored sign that read "The Wave" was front and center and a few feet above the entrance. The club was a local favorite and acted as a meeting place for all the spring breakers and high school kids of Bridgetown, Barbados. The club sat on the beach, and warm sand covered the ground rather than a typical dancefloor. Caribbean music blasted from the speakers, and luminous lights filled the venue. It felt like a constant euphoria as the young crowd raved to the sounds of Caribbean-styled techno music. All the young faces were glowing with sweat beads, and their bodies were drenched. It mostly came from the humid air. However, the rampant drug use added to the profuse perspiration. The DJ sat on a stage front and center that slightly towered over the crowd. He bopped back and forth, pumping his fist while controlling the group. The constant rhythmic drums that mimicked a speeding heartbeat kept everyone's adrenaline pumping.

Trey, a young man just nearing the age of sixteen, stood against the wall and watched as everyone around him seemed as if they were in a psychedelic trance. Small locs were tied at the top of his head while two strands dangled over his right eye. Trey felt uneasy and out of place as his eyes timidly scanned the room, studying the town's "in" crowd. He had been on the island for a few summers but never really fit in.

His mother, Aries, was adamant about them keeping a low profile. However, that night he was finally invited by one of his classmates, Jalen. He was a local youngster that took a liking to him. Jalen was the wanna-be bad boy and had a reputation in the town for being sheisty.

Trey felt a tap on his elbow, and he quickly looked to the left. Trey focused on the young boy beside him; it was Jalen Croswell.

"Yo, my big bro just texted me. He's ready for us to come in the back," Jalen said as he smiled and rubbed his hands together excitedly. Jalen threw his head towards the back, where Crow and his crew usually partied. It was off limits for everyone else, and that backroom had urban legends attached to it. Only the Crows got to go back there, and Jalen had been itching since his brother opened the club.

Jalen was a tall, slender kid with slight acne. His hair was nappy, and his sides were faded. He was fifteen as well and Trey's classmate. They had grown a friendship over the past year, and the more they hung out, the more Jalen learned about Trey's unique skillset; coding. All the gaming Trey did as a young boy prompted his mother to get him one-on-one lessons with some of Silicone Valley's rising stars. Well, it paid off because Trey was a technological beast. He was a prodigy and could break into anything digitally. He could build apps, websites, and whatever one would need. He was like an internet savant, and Jalen learned that quickly. Jalen never could get his older brother, Crow, to let him hang out with him and his crew, but he saw Trey as his way in.

"Are you sure about these guys?" Trey asked timidly as he began hearing his mother's voice telling him about making good decisions.

"Fa sho! These niggas are cool. It's my brother and his crew. You heard about them. The Murder of Crows?" Jalen said as he threw his arm around Trey's neck and walked through the sea of people.

"Yeah, everybody knows them," Trey replied as his eyes scanned the room while they made their way towards the back. The music was loud, so they had to yell to communicate.

"Exactly! I have been telling my brother all about you. How you can build sites and basically a computer God," Jalen said playfully as he smiled while looking at the scene, occasionally nodding and licking his lips when he made eye contact with girls.

Jalen was smooth and known as a ladies' man throughout their high school. This worked for him at school, but it worked against him when dealing with his brother, who was only a few years older. Crow, who was nineteen and a high school drop-out, was the leader of the young crew who terrorized the island. They robbed tourists, sold pills to the locals, and had been known for not fucking around.

Jalen's older brother's real name was Damon Croswell, but he simply went by Crow. He had an army of the town's dropouts, misfits, and savages under him, and they were all trained to go. Every teenager that the city threw away, Crow embraced them. He accepted them with open arms. He managed to take the town's scraps and mold them into a feared faction. They were like a family. They were all under eighteen and looked at their leader like a savior. They called themselves Murder of Crows, which meant a group of crows. The irony of it being called "A murder" fit into their reputation and infamy.

Trey and Jalen made it to the back door, and a sliding peephole was there. Jalen knocked on the door in a rhythmic pattern and looked back at the crowd and then at Trey. Jalen could tell Trey was nervous and placed his hand on his shoulder to reassure him.

"We are good, bro. He wants to meet you. I set it all up," Jalen confirmed.

"I'm good," Trey answered as he nodded his head in assurance. The small rectangular slot on the door slid open at that moment. A pair of buck eyes emerged through the slot, looking directly at them. Jalen through up his hands in frustration.

"Let me in nigga, damn," Jalen said with a smile.

The buck-eyed guy turned his head and said something to someone. Trey instantly noticed the initials M.O.C. on the young man's neck. The door opened, and Trey immediately felt the cold wind from the air-conditioned back portion. The guy at the door stepped to the side and cleared a pathway for the boys to enter. Jalen led the way, and Trey was close behind. The backroom was a completely different vibe. The room was dim, and a red light illuminated the makeshift lounge.

As Jalen and Trey walked through the room, they noticed comfortable sofas were lined against the wall. Small tables were placed in front of the couches full of pills and small mounds of cocaine. Trey couldn't believe what he was seeing. This was all new to him. He had seen classmates smoke weed behind the school but never hardcore drugs. Girls were all around, and some were naked, which excited the young boys.

Jalen and Trey looked at each other and giggled as a slim, tall blonde with two big melons swung back and forth. Her areoles were the size of bologna slices and blew their minds. She plopped on the couch, titties bouncing like basketballs, and the boys' eyes were locked in. She joined two other girls who were already on the couch. They all laughed, and then she did a nosedive into the pile of coke on the table. Trey's eyes were glued to her as he slowed his walk while turning his head. Jalen laughed and pulled him.

"Oh shit! Come on, man," Jalen said playfully as he laughed and put his fist to his mouth.

"This is like the matrix," Trey added, not believing what he was seeing. He focused on what was ahead of him. They followed the goon to what seemed to be another back door. The goon opened the door and waited for them to walk through. Jalen and Trey walked in, and the goon also stepped in, closing the door behind him. Trey immediately noticed that the sounds from the club was completely silenced. The spacious room was soundproof and cold. Trey instantly felt a chill go up his spine as he saw a group of men huddled around something. He paused and got scared, but almost instantly he felt a nudge in his back from the goon.

"Don't get scared now, lil' nigga. Gon' head..." the buck-eyed goon said.

As they got closer, they noticed what was happening. The party's feelings died quickly when they witnessed what was going on. A young, white boy with black, slicked back hair stuck out like a sore thumb amongst the island boys. The white guy looked twenty something years old and was the center of attention. He sat bound to a wooden chair with his hands tied behind his back. His face was bloody, and his shirt was drenched in sweat. Trey and Jalen were shocked as their mouths dropped at the scene unfolding before them. Trey's eyes fell on the white boy's hand, and he noticed the redness of his wrist from being in bondage. Trey's heart began to pound, and he felt like it was about to jump out of his chest. He had never seen anything like that.

"What the fuck is going on, bro?" Trey said to Jalen under his breath, trying not to move his lips while talking.

"Man, I don't know. He ain't say shit about this," Jalen said, leaning into Trey to hear his exasperated whisper. A raspy, deep voice emerged and Crow kneeled in front of the white boy with a menacing glare. Crow grabbed the white boy by his hair and lifted it, making sure the new guest saw his bludgeoned face.

Crow was shirtless, and his body was lean and completely ripped. His skin was deep black and smooth, showing no flaws. He was so dark; he almost looked purple. His head was bald and shiny. There was no hair on his body, giving him a distinctive look. He had no eyebrows, so his smooth face just blended in with his head. He was like no one that Trey had ever seen before. Crow suffered from Alopecia; a disease that prevented hair growth. His smooth, baby face and gray piercing eyes were intimidating. He had pure gold teeth with diamonds, adding to his grim look. His neck also had the initials M.O.C. On his chest was a gigantic crow tattoo; its wings expanding from one of Crow's shoulders to the other.

"Aht... aht don't be scared now. Ya'll want tu' play with de' big boys, eh?" Crow said as the island's accent dripped from his every word. He slowly stood to his feet with a smug smile. He looked at the two newcomers and locked eyes with Trey. Crow stared at him intensely. Although Trey was spooked to death, he didn't look away from Crow. He had heard so many stories about him, so he knew what to expect— a motherfucking monster.

Crow walked directly in front of Trey and never broke his stare. He began to talk to his brother but never looked Jalen's way. He wanted to size Trey up.

"So, dis de' brethren you wan' tu bring tu me?" Crow probed.

"Yeah, this my boy. He's official, bro. This mu'fucka can do anything you need. He a mu'fuckin genius. I'm telling you," Jalen responded confidently, not having a heavy accent like his brother.

"Official, eh?" Crow said as a slow smile spread across his face.

"Yeah, he's nice," Jalen confirmed.

"Okay, let's see," Crow said as he reached his hand back and wiggled his fingers.

Seconds later, one of the goons handed Crow a cell phone. He gave the cell phone to Trey and put his hand on his shoulder.

"This punk-ass white boy tried tu' come to buy some pills. Me don't like white boys, though," Crow said as he looked back and smiled. His crew all burst into laughter as Crow taunted him. "He won't budge. He is stubborn as an Ox. Me a give em' credit fa that," Crow said as he stepped even closer to Trey. He was so close that their foreheads were touching. Crow was slightly taller than Trey, so he towered over him and looked down. "Open his phone," Crow said as he handed Trey the cell.

Trey took a deep breath and grabbed the cell phone. He instantly touched a few buttons, and then he reset it. Everyone was focused on Trey as he worked his magic. Trey waited for the phone to turn back on, and the phone was unlocked just like that.

"Told you... this nigga the truth," Jalen said as he stuck out his chest. His arrogance was showing all over his face as he looked around the circle of Crows. Jalen threw his arm around Trey and started talking that talk.

"This nigga like Steve Jobs or some shit. He can

get into any phone, system, or tech shit. I don't know what that shit called, but this nigga can do it," Jalen stated arrogantly.

"Yu' fucked up, eh?" Crow said as he grabbed the boy's hair and pulled, asking him to look Crow directly in the eyes.

"Go tu' his cash app," Crow said as he aggressively pushed the boy's head and released, ridding it from his grip.

"Alright," Trey said as he did what he was told. Crow walked over to Trey and looked down at the phone as he opened the app.

"Oh, yu' have a lot of paper," Crow said jokingly. He was shocked at the amount of cash in his cash app. "Send it tu' me," Crow said as he grabbed the phone and typed in his handle.

"You might not want to do that," Trey said timidly, not knowing if he should've spoken. Crow's aura was very intimidating and menacing. Trey had never been around people of the underworld. He immediately regretted speaking up as he felt the animosity directed towards him.

"Huh...what de' fuck do yu' mean?" Crow said as he frowned up. His facial expression signaled his whole crew to get closer to Trey, ready to give him the beating of his life. Trey was shaking. It seemed like the walls were closing in.

"It's traceable, meaning it can be traced right back to you. You might want to transfer it by Bitcoin," Trey said as his voice cracked and trembled. He was nervous and was doing a horrible job hiding it.

"Bitcoin? What de' fuck is dat?" Crow said as he grew annoyed by Trey's suggestion. Fuck a Bitcoin. He wanted that money in his account so he had immediate access to it.

"A type of digital currency in which a record of transactions is maintained, and new units of currency are generated by the computational solution of mathematical problems, and which operates independently of a central bank," Trey explained.

"Whoa, hold dat nerd talk. Make dat shit simple," Crow said as he was confused at the information that Trey just laid on him.

"That shit federal. Shit gon' have them alphabet boys on yo ass," Jalen interjected, trying to help his brother understand Trey.

"If I was you, I would turn that money into Bitcoin and then send it to yourself," Trey said.

"Ahh," Crow said as he cracked a smile and began slow bobbing, somewhat understanding what Trey was trying to explain. "Dirty money... clean hands. I like de' way yu' think."

"I told you my nigga cold," Jalen interjected.

Crow handed the phone back to Trey. Crow was looking at Trey as he converted the money. He still didn't understand the concept, so he figured he'd cover his ass.

"Send it to yu'self, and I'll get it from yu'," Crow instructed as he gave Trey a look that said he wasn't taking no for an answer.

"Oh... okay," Trey stuttered, feeling like he was doing something wrong by agreeing to do what Crow asked.

He pushed a few buttons quickly and precisely. After about a minute of focusing on the screen, he lifted his head and handed Crow the phone.

"All done," he said with a sense of pride. He had transferred the money to himself and then to Crow. "Clean money," he added. Crow slowly took the phone and saw the transaction to himself.

"Clean money," Crow repeated as he held his fist towards Trey. Trey looked down and smiled at Crow's sentiment, and fist bumped him. The feeling of acceptance overcame him, which was something Trey had been searching for ever since he and his mother came to the islands.

"Told you! My nigga the truth, mu'fucka!" Jalen said as he walked around, looking at the Crows as if they were peasants. He finally had something to be proud of. He had been thirsting to become a part of his brother's crew for years. He saw this as an opportunity to show his value to the crew.

Crow walked over to the kid tied to the chair, hocked up saliva, and spat on the boy.

"Let 'em' go," Crow said as he looked down at the boy in anger. The crew gasped and sounds of the displeasure of his decision erupted. His crew waited on a chance to tear his ass up. His audacity to come to buy drugs from him without backup. He felt offended.

"Now!" Crow yelled, sending chills up everyone's backs with his tone. He had established fear into the hearts of his crew. They knew that he would go to the extreme to prove a point or if he felt disrespected. Crow was an animal.

One of the members untied the young man, and Crow got off on the fear he caused. He could see in the young man's eyes that he was scared shitless.

"Go," Crow calmly said as he threw his head towards the door. Almost instantly, the guy took off and out of the door, thankful that he still had his life. Crow then focused his attention on Trey. He stuck out his fist to give Trey a pound. Crow smiled, showing his bright, golden slugs. Even when he smiled, he still looked demented. Trey pounded Crow's hand and smiled as well. Jalen held out his hand, and Crow slapped it away, making everyone laugh at Jalen's expense.

"Man, let's go," Jalen said as he felt small amongst laughter. He and Trey left out and joined the party again. Crow watched as they left and then looked back at the phone, seeing the money in his account.

"Me like de' young brethren. Keep an eye on him, eh," Crow demanded his crew.

Chapter Two

SAINTS AND DEVILS

"Man, I'm telling you... that's her! I swear to God, bruh," a teenage boy said as they sat on the sands of the beach.

A small island food spot was about twenty feet away. He was in a small huddle with his friends. It was three boys, all around fifteen years old with their beach shorts on, topless. They were trying to figure out if they were looking at one of the legends that they had seen on YouTube and a few docuseries. They tried to remain discreet, hoping that she wouldn't mind them admiring her from far. Her beautiful, sun kissed skin and grace was mesmerizing to the young crew. Her slim shape and soft features had the boys in awe. She wore an earth toned sundress with a matching ebony-toned headwrap, just barely displaying her baby hairs resting neatly on her edges. She waited the four occupied tables effortlessly, all with a warming smile and hospitality. She skillfully maneuvered with plates in both of her hands, holding them high as she made her way to the back entrance to the kitchen.

Just before she reached the back door, she paused and shot a piercing look at the boys, immediately making them tense up. They didn't know what to do as she stared at them with a menacing demeanor. She playfully stuck out her tongue and then kissed her wrist, where a noticeable tattoo was. It was tattooed initials that read "MM." The boys noticed it too and a wave of fear overcame them.

One of the boys ran in the opposite direction and the other two shortly followed. Aries chuckled to herself and laughed as she made her way into the house.

"Trey, how long for dem oxtails for table four, eh?" Aries said as she placed the plates in her hand inside the dishwasher. She washed her hands over the sink and looked over at her son who was stirring the red cast iron pot, peeking down at the juicy oxtails that were submerged in red and green peppers, all while swimming in a tub of brown gravy.

"They're done, Ma," Trey answered quickly as he wore a white apron and a busboy uniform underneath. They were a family business; a two-man crew, who held down the restaurant known as Robyn's. Aries had named the small boutique restaurant after her now deceased sister.

"Okay gud. Now, go check dem jerk chicken," Aries instructed as she threw her head in the direction of the smoking grill just left of the outside dining area. Trey rolled his eyes and headed in the direction of the exit. Aries noticed.

"Hey, what's that?" Aries asked as she stopped him in his tracks by gently grabbing his arm. "Me no need any attitude, Trey. You have to help mommy out, ok?" Trey's head was down and his locs were covering his eyes. Aries then took two fingers and placed them under his chin. She slightly lowered her head, trying to see his eyes through the sea of hair.

"Ok?" she repeated.

"Yea, I know, Ma," Trey said as he looked at his mother's beautiful eyes and slightly grinned.

"Ok den. Go on," she ordered as she watched him make his way outside and tended to the grill. Aries leaned back on the sink and folded her arms, admiring her son and how he had grown up so quickly. He was now taller than her and she began to feel guilty. She understood that he was a teenage boy and needed to have a social life. However, she needed him to work at the restaurant with her on the weekends to accommodate the rush of tourists.

"Where did the time go?" she said as she smiled and reached into her apron.

A perfectly rolled joint was tucked and waiting for her inside. She quickly grabbed it, along with her weed, and sparked up. She took two deep drags of the ganja and held the smoke in her chest. She threw her head back and closed her eyes as she let the smoke dance in his lungs, then she slowly exhaled. She blew a cloud of smoke into the air and then peeked outside, seeing that one of her favorites on the island approached.

It was a young girl in her early twenties. Her face was friendly and she had fair skin with big, deep, brown eyes. Her pupils were big like a baby doll and small brown freckles were scattered over her nose and cheeks. Her sandy brown hair was extremely thick and not well maintained. The wildness of her hair had an uncanny beauty to it though. She was a free soul and you could tell as soon as you laid eyes on her. This girl was different. She was special, literally. Her name was Flower. It was a name she had adopted from the island folks.

A while back she had been found wandering the island with no claim to her. The sheriff tried to help her, but it was hard to communicate with her because she was mute. Flower never said a word, ever. She had the mind capacity of a five-year-old and her mental was severely underdeveloped.

It seemed as if she came out of nowhere. The sheriff assumed that family members from a nearby island didn't want her and just let her wander off. Caring for a special needs person could be daunting, however, no one could quite understand how someone could throw away a wonderful soul like Flower. It was their loss... but a big gain for the small town called Bridgetown.

After weeks of trying to find out if someone or a family had been searching for a missing loved one... no one came forward. So, the town stepped in as a collective and took her in as one of their own. No one directly took care of her, but everyone did their part to help with her. No one really knew how she got the name, but it just stuck. No one knew her birthname, so Flower it was.

The sheriff let Flower stay in one of the holding cells at night since the local crime was non-existent and they had no better use for the space. Sure sometimes the sheriff had to toss a drunk in the cell overnight to sober up, which took her room away. But for the most part, she had made it her home. Aries had taken a liking to her and would feed her every day and in return, Flower would bring her a flower or two. It was a perfect trade every time for Aries. Flower would hand out flowers to the patrons of the restaurant and it gave the place a feeling of comfort. She was becoming a local legend and Aries was her number one supporter.

"Hey, gyal!" Aries said as she stepped out of the door and watched as Flower walked around to each of the outside tables and placed a flower on it. She had on a sundress that one of the local vendors gifted her and it had big side pockets. Just enough room for Flower to stuff about a dozen flowers in each side. Aries smiled and called to her again. This time, it caught Flower's attention. She looked at Aries and smiled from ear to ear. She clapped her hands in excitement and stood on her tip toes in glee. Aries was her favorite person on the island and it showed by the way her face lit up every time she saw her.

"Good morning, sunshine," Aries said as she approached Flower and gave her a big kiss on the cheek. Flower accepted the kiss and squinted her eyes as her big cheeks rose while smiling.

"What kind of flowers do we have today?" Aries asked as she looked down at her hands. Flower immediately dug into her side pocket and pulled out the flower. She extended her arms, handing one to Aries. Aries received the flower and looked at it while grinning.

"Ohh, okay... okay! We got sunflowers today, eh?" Aries exclaimed as she examined the big, yellow petals and long stems. Flower frantically shook her head up and down, confirming the flower type.

"Where yu' get dese' from, eh? Hope not from Mr. Johnson's yard. Yu' know he's old and grumpy." Aries playfully pinched Flower's cheek and then winked at her. "Just don't get caught," Aries said. Aries took another puff of her joint and then put it out on one of the ashtrays on the table.

"I think they're beautiful," Aries added as she twirled the stem, making the flower spin around. Flower giggled and repeatedly clapped her hands playfully. Flower then began to place the flowers on the table as Aries dressed the tables with silverware, preparing for the first wave of tourists that would be arriving at any minute.

Aries quickly did a double take at the unfamiliar face. Aries returned to the kitchen and after a few moments, she saw that she had her first guest. She walked out to greet the man. She immediately knew that he wasn't a tourist because of his tan; his demeanor, and the fact that he wasn't falling down drunk. Her customers commonly ended up tipsy by the time they reached her establishment. Tourists usually couldn't resist the row of bars that lined the coastline. The man had on linen shorts with an open linen shirt to match. His slightly bulging belly was on full display and the bucket hat he had on covered half of his face. Aries could only see his full beard and lips from afar. She stepped out and greeted him with a big smile.

"Welcome to Robyn's," she said while walking towards him. The man was looking down at his phone and whatever he was looking at commanded all his attention. Aries slowly approached him and then repeated herself. But not before letting out a sarcastic cough, clearing her throat.

"Welcome to Robyn's," she repeated but now she was standing over him with her arms crossed.

He locked eyes with her and simply responded, "Thank you," just before he returned to looking down at his phone. When he talked, Aries instantly noticed his bottom rows of gold teeth. His top row was perfectly aligned and white. Aries immediately thought he was handsome; however, his arrogant attitude made him ugly in her eyes.

"Do you know what you want?" Aries asked, getting slightly annoyed by his nonchalant demeanor. The man looked up at Aries and paused, staring at her. He didn't notice her beauty until that moment.

"Nah. What's good here?"

"Everything is good," Aries responded as she shifted her weight to one side and placed her hands on her hips.

"I'll take the rice and beans... and the jerk," Saint said as he placed his phone on the table and folded his hands just over it. Aries paused and squinted her eyes.

"What did yu' come here for?" she asked in a cautious tone. Saint smiled.

"What do you mean? I came here to eat," he answered.

"Well, yu' ordered without looking at the menu. Also, we don't have website, so obviously yu' planned dis trip to me establishment. Me never forget a face and yu' have never been here before," Aries retorted.

"Damn... you good, love," Saint confessed as he

shook his head and smiled. He was impressed by her observation skills. She saw right through him and he had to come clean.

"So, what are yu' here for?" Aries continued as her guards were up. She tried to study his face and see if she could recognize him from her previous life back in the States. She had done so many bad things in her past, she always was on high alert for her karma.

"I'm Saint. I was wondering if we could do some business?" Saint asked as he slightly lifted his bucket hat so that she could see his eyes.

"Me not interested," Aries quickly responded after she rolled her eyes and instantly regretted wasting as much time as she did with homeboy.

"All due respect, but you haven't even heard my proposition," Saint said as he sat back in his chair and folded his hands. Aries looked at the mysterious man in confusion. She felt the urge to reach into her apron and wrap her pointer finger around the trigger of her small caliber gun. She kept studying the man's face and he didn't look familiar as she quickly jogged her memory. Aries never forgot a face. She was almost sure that she had never ran across him before.

"Look, me no have no time fa games, yu' hear?" Aries said, now growing angrier with his persistent attempts to play mental gymnastics with her.

"I'm definitely not playing games with you, love. That's not what I'm about at all. Just tryna talk commerce with you. See if we can build."

"Well, me not interested. Also, we are closed for lunch," Aries said as she scooped up his menu.

"Okay, I see that I rubbed you the wrong way. My apologies," he said as he slowly stood up and stepped closer to Aries. He towered over her and looked down at her pretty eyes. His eyes were piercing, but they were kind. He wasn't trying to be intimidating, but he wanted to make sure she was the only one who could hear him.

"Hear me out," he whispered. She could smell his fresh cologne and the shea butter on his full beard. He then whispered.

"I can change your life. I just need help cleaning up some money, feel me? Fifty racks a month goes directly in your pocket. That's how much I got for you to make me a partner here. I invest some money in the spot, make some renovations... plush this mu'fucka out. Then you cut me a monthly check until we reach three million."

Aries instantly laughed and scoffed at the numbers. He was doing the very thing that she had been doing for years and that was cleaning dirty money. Aries had financial security already, so the numbers he was talking were pennies to her. The fact that he approached her out of all people humored her.

"Good day, Mr. Saint," Aries said as she turned her back and walked towards the back entrance. She stopped by the other guest and kindly spoke.

"Come on, Flower," she said just before she disappeared into the kitchen and flipped the open sign to closed, leaving Saint standing there, stuck. Aries waited for Flower and then she ushered her into the house and followed close behind. Aries looked back at Saint just before she closed the door and rolled her eyes at him. She didn't like his proposition, not one bit. She was supposed to be hiding out, living a low-key life. She didn't need any unwanted attention on her or her family. She was over it.

He smiled, knowing that Aries was going to be a tough task. It wasn't every day that someone turned down that much money. This instantly made him intrigued by the island girl.

"Love feisty as hell. How I'm posed to get her to see shit my way?" he asked himself as he stared at the closed sign. He shook his head, got up, and placed a hundred-dollar bill under the coffee cup. He slowly walked away, looking forward to the challenge of gaining Aries' interest. His mind was set and Saint always found a way to conquer the things that he focused on.

***

Aries sat on her balcony and watched the stars. She swiftly ran her tongue along the wrapping paper, then twisted up the OG Kush that filled it. She sparked the ganja and took a deep pull, sending the smoke into her lungs, and held it there. She closed her eyes as she felt the smoke dancing in her chest. Her full lips puckered and then she slowly blew out the smoke, hoping that some of the stress left out along with it.

The impromptu visit from Saint really shook her. She wasn't just an ordinary business owner. She was a retired killer and trying to hide from her past and live a low-key life. It seemed as if all of that changed the moment Saint sat at her establishment. Not to mention, she was on an FBI wanted list back home. With Miamor still in prison, she was the only one who made it out, so the threat of anything coming to disrupt that had her on edge. She didn't know if this nigga was a fed, an extortionist, or just a hustler trying to clean up money. Whichever he was, she wanted no part of it. She took another pull of the smoke. She decided that she would revert to her old ways if Saint ever put her in a position to disrupt the safe haven she had created for her and Trey.

She heard someone enter her bedroom and she instinctively grabbed her snub nose that was under the stand next to her. She quickly spun around and pointed it at the male that was approaching her from the rear. Her heart dropped when she saw who it was.

"Mom!" Trey said as he stopped in his tracks and put his hands up in fear. He looked at the gun with his mother's hands wrapped around it. A wave of guilt overcame Aries as she lowered her gun and instantly began to apologize.

"Trey, my baby. Mommy is so sorry," she said as her eyes traveled to his shaking hands. He had never seen a gun before. Let alone, having one pointed at him. He was frozen in fear. Aries was a very strong woman; however, seeing the fear on Trey's worried face instantly broke her. Tears welted up in her eyes as she put the gun away and then placed a hand over her mouth as her emotions took over her. She kept thinking that the old her would have shot first and asked questions later; possibly killing her son. The thoughts of that were too much for her to hold inside as the tears ran down her face and then her hand.

"You have a gun?" Trey asked, not understanding seeing his mother in that type of zone.

"I'm so sorry, baby," she hesitantly replied with a shaky voice.

Trey had never seen that look in her eyes before. He was looking at the window to the soul of a cold killer. In the game that she came from, she was a legend. Aries stood up and hugged her son tightly, knowing that he didn't know that he had almost lost his life. The old her had clicked on and she thanked God that she hesitated before pulling the trigger. Years ago, that would have never happened. Never. She knew that it would be a pain that she would've never gotten over. She instantly understood she had to handle the Saint situation and she had to do it fast. He was tearing down the wall that she had built around her son and she wasn't having it. For the first time in years, she felt the Murder Mama in her resurfacing, rearing its ugly head.

Chapter Three

FIRECRACKER

With all my heart, I love you, baby
Stay with me and you will see
My arms will hold you, baby
Never leave, 'cause I believe I'm in love
Sweet love... Sweet Love

Lovey swayed her wide hips back and forth as she sang along to Anita Baker. The speakers were louder than usual but her song came on and it deserved its proper respect. She stood over the stove, fried up bacon, and browned the hash browns. Her silver hair was tied loosely into a bun and sweat beads were on her nose and forehead. Her wide hips filled out the baby blue apron and her big legs were like tree stumps. However, her seventy-one years looked good on her.

It was just before sunrise and she was preparing breakfast for her favorite guy in the world, Saint. It was a weekday, so she didn't have to worry about feeding guests, being they ran a luxury bed and breakfast spot. The guests slept on the west wing, while Saint and Lovey resided on the east. Lovey was in the zone and she felt good that morning. Her arthritis wasn't bothering her and Pandora radio was on a roll. She tried to hit Anita's notes as she picked up the pan from off the stove and slid the potatoes onto a plate. She didn't even notice Saint leaning against the wall with his arms folded. He was bare chested and he had on long pajama pants, just waking up from his night's slumber. He couldn't help but smile and watch as she enjoyed herself. She looked over at Saint and she jumped, startled by his presence. They both burst into laughter and Lovey showed that big, beautiful smile that always made Saint feel warm inside. Her golden-brown skin and scattered freckles just under both of her eyes made her one of a kind.

"Boy, you scared the shit outta me," she said playfully as she put the skillet down.

"Lovey, I thought you said you was gon' stop cussin' so much," Saint pleaded as he walked towards her.

"God ain't through with me yet. I'm a work in progress," Lovey responded as she held her cheek out. Saint walked up to her and laid a kiss on her big cheeks. He then walked over to the table and took a seat. He looked towards the door and saw Crow sitting on the porch, watching as people walked up and down the street.

"I see you didn't invite Crow in... again," Saint said sarcastically as he jokingly squinted his eyes at Lovey. Saint paid Crow to watch the house while he slept. Some would say it was extreme, but Saint was naturally paranoid. He rewarded Crow good money and it was just a part of the job. Saint understood his position at the top of the totem pole, so he went to the max to protect himself and the only woman that he loved; Lovey. Crow was the only one on the island that Saint trusted outside of her. He was like a ghost within the town and he did that purposely. He just wanted to clean his money and live legit from here on out.

"You know I don't care for that boy. I don't what it is, but I just don't trust em," she said as she placed the breakfast in front of Saint.

"Come on, he ain't that bad," Saint said as he smiled, showing his flawless white teeth.

"I know the devil when I see him," Lovey said as she glanced over at him and a chill went up her spine. His hairless face creeped her out and his pupils seemed soulless to her.

"Well love, even the devil is useful in hell," Saint said as he took a bite of his toast and winked at Lovey.

"Boy hush, talking that foolishness in the house. This is a God-fearing home," Lovey said as she smiled back and playfully hit him with the dry towel. "Now, hurry the hell up so I can finish cleaning my kitchen," Lovey added, sending them both into laughter because of her dirty mouth.

Saint finished up his food and stepped outside where Crow was sitting.

"Top of the top," Saint said as he stepped out, rubbing his stomach.

"Morning, big homie," Crow responded as Saint sat and joined him on the stoop.

"Go and get you some rest," Saint instructed, knowing that Crow had worked third shift, protecting his home.

"Me, no sleep. Sleep is cousin of death, eh?" Crow said, smiling as he reached out his hand and slapped palms with Saint. They both looked forward at nothing. Local business owners were setting up their shops, preparing for the new wave of daily tourists that came through. The cruise ships provided a steady flow of foot traffic and was the main source of commerce for the island.

"A lil' birdy told me somebody got touched up the other night at the club," Saint said as he ran his tongue across the top row of his mouth and sucked his teeth. Crow noticed that Saint's words were playful but the expression was not. It showed agitation as the muscles in his jaws were clenched.

"Dat was nuttin, yu' heard? Just a little white boy, we had to touch up," Crow explained.

"A local?" Saint asked.

"Nah, out of towner."

"Keep that shit out of my club. I asked you to run it and stay out of the way. That lil' petty-young shit will crumble everything I got going," Saint said as he stayed looking forward, making himself clear without even giving Crow the respect of eye contact.

"Listen, what you know about the chick that got that jerk shack by the docks? The little wooden spot with the smokers that people be lined up at?" Saint asked, thinking about his encounter with her the day prior.

"Robyn's?" Crow responded, knowing exactly where he was talking about. It was by far the most popular food spot on the island and it seemed like it happened overnight. The smoke and charcoal smell always attracted the tourists.

"Yeah, that's it," Saint answered.

"Me don't know too much. Island gal don't fuck wit' no one. She stay out de' way."

"What nigga behind her?" Saint asked.

"No one that me know about," said Crow.

"Well… check this out. Need you and the lil homies to go over there and make some noise. Not too bad though. Just want to shake her up a little. Understand me?"

Crow smiled and nodded his head in understanding. He loved terrorizing shit and when Saint sent an order down, Crow was always ready to show his importance to him.

"One through ten?" Crow asked, referring to the severity of the shake down. Saint looked at Crow, established eye contact, and made sure he understood what he was about to say.

"One," he stated. Crow nodded his head in understanding. Saint then put his hand on his shoulder and repeated himself.

"One," Saint reiterated.

Saint was taught a long time ago, if you wanted a person to fully understand what you were saying, you had to put your hand on them. This ideology could be used in a variety of things, and Saint was a student of this philosophy.

Saint stood up and gave Crow a pound before disappearing back into the house. Crow headed to the spot to gather a couple members of his crew then…. Aries.

***

"Come back and see me, eh," Aries said as she picked up the cash that sat on the table and slipped it in the front pocket of her apron. She then picked up the plates that had nothing but chicken bones on them. Two satisfied customers had just demolished her famous jerk chicken and cabbage. The older couple both smiled and prepared to leave. That's when Flower approached them with two beautiful, lavender colored tulips. They accepted the flowers gracefully and the older gentlemen dug into his pockets. He gave Flower a few quarters, dimes, and nickels. Flower's face lit up in glee as she stood on her tippy toes and clapped so fast. She was genuinely happy about that loose change. Aries stopped at the door that led to the kitchen, looking back at Flower doing what she usually does.

"Come on, gyal!" Aries said as she gave a big smile and chuckled to herself. She threw her head in the direction of the door. Flower immediately skipped to Aries and they entered the kitchen.

Trey was in the kitchen over the sink. He was mixing chicken with jerk seasoning, moving his hands and fingers throughout the meat.

"Make sure yu' squeeze some lime in that, Trey," Aries instructed, knowing that was a small step that Trey would often forget.

"I got it, Mom," Trey said with a tad bit of annoyance in his voice.

"Nigga, what yu' got in yu' chest? Yu' want trouble?" Aries said playfully as she smiled.

It was the little things that Aries' father taught her that made her chicken amazing. This automatically made her think to a time when she was younger and naïve to the life's ills that the island had to offer.

"Maaa," Trey whined as he turned his head, not looking into his mom's beautiful eyes. He couldn't help but return the smile as it forced its way onto his face. Flower let out a small chuckle as she covered her mouth. Both of their heads shot to Flower, being that they never really heard her make a verbal noise.

"Yu' think that's funny, eh?" Aries said and she smiled even bigger. She took that as a sign that Flower really, really trusted them. It warmed Aries' heart as she loosened Trey's collar and walked over to Flower. Flower instantly folded her hands into one another and looked down, avoiding contact with Aries. She still had the grin on her face from Aries' play fight with Trey.

"Yu' comfortable round' here, ain't yu,' gyal?" Aries asked as she took her pointer finger and gently placed it under Flower's chin. She slighted raised Flower's chin so they were eye to eye. Flower's eyes shifted from left to right, avoiding eye contact; however, the grin was still present.

Out of nowhere, the sounds of plates being broken and loud noises were just outside the back door. The sounds seemed close and it was so noisy no one could ignore it. The sounds of tables scrapping against the concrete sounded through the air. Aries and Trey instantly went to the back to see what was going on.

"What de' fuck!" Aries screamed as she saw five men destroying her patio where her customers sat and ate. They were all young boys with a head full of dreads and sun kissed brown skin. All of them were active, except one. He was black as tar, slim, and bald. It was Crow. He stood there with a small pocketknife in one hand and a mango in the other. He leaned against Aries and cut small pieces and ate them as if he didn't have a care in the world as the crew tore up Aries' establishment. Trey ran up on one of the men and they pushed him, crashing him into a table, causing him to fall onto the ground and whimper. He held his side in pain and Aries went crazy. She ran over to the guy and scratched his face with her hands, digging her nails into his forehand and forcefully dragging them down to his chin. He instantly began to bleed and screamed. She followed it up with an onslaught of slaps to his face. She was enraged.

"Don't yu' ever in yo' motherfuckin' life touch me son... yu' pussy boy!" Aries screamed as she stepped back and watched the scratches spewing blood.

The island boy raised his hand back about to smack fire from Aries, but he felt a strong hand catch his as he prepared to strike. The island boy looked back and it was Crow.

"Calm! Calm!" He ordered as he looked into the eyes of his henchmen. The irate island boy instantly eased up and Crow released his arm. Crow whistled loudly, causing everyone to stop in their tracks and then all eyes were on him. It was as if they were dogs, obeying their master's call to yield. He had them trained and militant. The Crows were a terror.

The island boy grabbed his face and wiped the blood away as he breathed heavily, making his chest go up and down speedily. Crow focused on

55

Aries, who was on fire with anger. He knew that they couldn't touch her because of the specific instructions from Saint. He smiled sinisterly as she stepped to him. Crow looked down on her and they both said nothing. Crow grew a small smirk on his face, admiring her bravery.

"Yu' are bra—" Crow began to talk but was interrupted by a giant wad of spit flying into his face. Aries had denigrated him to the fullest as she stood toe to toe with him. Crow kept the grin on his face as he wiped the spit from his face and focused back on Aries.

"What de' fuck is dis, eh? You obviously don't know who de' fuck I am," Aries said, meaning every word wholeheartedly.

He couldn't have known. If he did, he would have thought twice about doing what he just did to her place. Aries had killed people for less before. And although she had been a murderer for hire in her past life, it categorized her as a serial killer theoretically. She was a motherfucking Murder Mama and her trigger finger began to itch. Crow saw her hand move and he looked lower, seeing that she had a .22 caliber gun pointed to his gut. Water was in her eyes, not because she was sad but because she was so on fire and furious. She wanted to give Crow a couple of hot ones in his belly SO

BAD. Crow saw that her trigger finger was on the trigger and her hand was steady, letting him know that she was comfortable with gunplay.

Crow held up his hands as if he was a hostage and continued to smile.

"Whoa… whoa. Me just here to deliver a message. This isn't personal, firecracker," he said, giving Aries a nickname. Crow continued his message.

"It's business," he said.

Aries lowered her gun and now it was on his dick. She dug the barrel into his balls so he could feel the iron. Crow's body tensed up. He had a gut feeling that Aries would blow her gun, so his smile was now a look of concern.

"Who fuckin' sent yu'? Whoever it was… yu' tell him I'll send his mudda to him in a box," Aries promised.

"Saint. He wanted me to tell yu' to tink about de' offer again," Crow said. Aries instantly grew even more upset. The fact that Saint had the balls to send someone to her spot to shake her down was appalling.

"Well, yu' tell him, me have an offer for him. Me going to tell him that personally though," Aries said, beginning to put a play in her mind. This caused her to smile. They just didn't fucking know.

They didn't fucking know.

"I'll deliver de' message, firecracker," Crow said as he slowly stepped back with his hands still up.

Aries watched him closely as she really thought about making a scene but the Murder Mama in her knew that wasn't the right move. She was in hiding and any attention could cause her something greater than proving a point to a naïve local trying to play gangster. She instantly realized that the crew were little ignorant boys. She could call her nephew CJ from Miami to tear all their asses up and shake up the town. She shook her head and looked back at Trey, who was still on the ground in shock.

"Get up, Trey," she ordered as she reached her hand out to assist him. "Are yu' ok?" she asked with a concerned look on her face. Her mommy mode crept in and the fury subsided.

"Yeah, I'm good," he said as he clutched his stomach and looked at Crow in confusion.

"It was just a misunderstanding, youngster," Crow said as his form of apology to Trey.

"Come on," Aries said as she threw her arm around Trey and guided him to the back door so they could return inside. Aries looked up and saw Flower standing at the door trembling as she nervously fiddled with her fingers. A huge wet spot was on her dress and it was clear that she had pissed herself. Tears were in her eyes and she was extremely terrified. Aries' heart dropped seeing Flower like that. She knew that she didn't understand what was fully going on and the ruckus had scared her to the point that she couldn't control her bodily functions.

"Let's get yu' cleaned up, gyal," Aries said as she shook her head in disgust. She looked back at Crow and noticed he and his crew were leaving. It took all her willpower not to send bullets into their backs. However, her time as a Murder Mama taught her the art of time and patience. You see, revenge is a dish best served cold. Not in a sense of being cold-hearted or unsympathetic but the ability to not eat your prey so quickly. You must let the plate get cold... let it cool off. Then act. That's what a true queen was; the ability to see things a few steps ahead. Specifically, a cartel queen.

Chapter Four

RUN THIS TOWN

Saint wiped the cold out of his eye as he walked down the hall. Just like every morning, he smelled the food, and the sounds of old R& B coming from downstairs. Lovey never missed a day of cooking and setting the mood for the house. Saint heard laughing and instantly grew suspicious. Lovey never had company in the house and the sound was unfamiliar to him. He made his way downstairs and what he saw really confused him. His grandmother sat at the kitchen table with a woman and he didn't know what to think or how to react. He entered the space and their conversation stopped immediately.

"Well, look what de' cat drug in," Aries said as she sat in the chair that Saint usually sat in for his morning breakfast. Saint halfway smiled and his eyes burrowed in confusion.

"Wha...what are you doing here?" he asked as

he walked over to Lovey and stood above her. He didn't want to alarm his grandmother, so he played it cool. But he knew that he wasn't on the best terms with Aries because of him sending his little niggas to her spot and trashing it.

"Hey, sleepyhead. Just was here talking to this amazing woman on this fine morning," Aries said as she crossed her legs. She wore a natural-colored head wrap. Her nude oversized sundress showed no trace of her shape, just the print of her petite nipples that sat on petite breasts.

Saint was stuck, trying to put things together. He knew that he had just sent Crow and his crew at her the day before. He also realized that Crow was outside, standing post of his home. She looked back and saw Crow sitting on the porch through the glass.

"Good morning," he replied, not wanting to alarm Lovey. He sat down and joined the two at the table. He looked Aries directly in the eyes. She was steady— calm and he didn't see any retreat in her gaze. He didn't blink but neither did she.

"Ok, well, let me cook these eggs for you two. We've been waiting on you to get up so they would be fresh," Lovey said as she slowly stood up from the table, using her arm as a crutch, which helped her. She let out a small grunt on her rise. Saint and

Aries still stared, having a silent contest. On the other hand, Lovey had a gigantic grin on her face, loving the fact that they had a guest. The only visitor she was used to was Crow, and it was clear how she felt about him.

"Thanks, Lovey," Saint responded. He looked into the pretty, light colored eyes of Aries.

"No problem, baby. I know you two had a good night. You need breakfast to give you some fuel for the day," Lovey said as she looked at Saint and smiled.

"What you mean?" Saint said as he broke the stare and looked at his grandmother. He noticed her now smiling. She put her hands on her waist and turned her head slightly as if she was saying, *'I know what happened, child.'* Lovey was at a certain age where she was blunt and she didn't hold punches.

"Uhm hmm," she said as she turned back and started to crack the eggs. "I saw the way she was staring at you earlier this morning," she added.

"Earlier?" Saint asked, not understanding what Lovey was referring to.

"Hush yo' mouth, boy. You know what I'm talking bout," Lovey said followed by a small chuckle. She continued. "I came in there to put your clothes away and saw that girl standing over you. Just a smiling! She was glowing. Child! I miss those days when... whew, let me hush my mouth." Lovey wiggled her hips.

That's when Aries broke her stare and looked over at Lovey do her little dance. Aries laughed as well. However, she was laughing for another reason than Lovey. She saw the way Saint took a hard swallow and his eyes bulged slightly. That's the exact moment that Saint knew Aries was different. He was sitting across from a street legend; an urban myth. He was still confused though.

Who the fuck are you? he thought as he looked at her. He looked at the porch again and peeped Crow. He still didn't understand how she got past him. His heart was now beating fast and his chest heaved up and down.

"How do you like yo' eggs, baby?" Lovey questioned.

"It's okay, ma'am. Me don't eat eggs, but me will take some of those potatoes and fruit yu' got over dere'." Aries still was staring. She was ice cold. Saint then realized he was in a game of mental chess.

"Okay, baby, coming right up," Lovey replied enthusiastically. "Alexa, play my favorites!" Lovey yelled, looking towards the voice-activated speaker she had sitting on the counter.

I will love you anyway, even if you cannot stay
I think you are the one for me
Here is where you ought to be…

"Aye! Dis' me jam," Aries said as she raised her hands and snapped on rhythm. Lovey looked at Aries and continued singing as Aries vibed out with her. They both swung back and forth as Saint watched, getting more upset with each snap. He looked at Aries and couldn't believe her. He knew just by looking at her that she didn't have a hint of fear in her body language. Lovey danced as she made it over to Saint, placing a plate in front of him.

Don't' you know you're my everything… yes you are…

Lovey continued to sing and went to fix Aries' plate. Aries focused on Saint and whispered just a tad over the music so Saint could hear her, but low enough where Lovey couldn't.

"Don't yu' ever play wit' me, eh," she instructed with a look of murder. If looks could kill, Saint would've been lined in chalk right there in that kitchen. She paused and her jaws tightened as she clenched her teeth tightly. "Ever," she added. She then looked over at Lovey who had started washing the pans and wasn't looking their way.

Aries reached under her dress and pulled out the same gun that she put to Crow's nuts. She sat the pistol on the table and had the barrel facing Saint. She calmly placed a cloth napkin over the top of it and concealed it. Saint shook his head and couldn't do anything but smile. He shook his head and had to admit she caught him slipping. He couldn't believe that a woman had did it. This is the same thinking that made her and her crew so feared back in the States. They came as the most unexpected treat and almost always hit their target. Saint was getting a master-level class on who the fuck Aries was.

"You got it. You got me," he admitted, talking in the same tone as she did. They were having this dark, sinister conversation all while Lovey was having a great time in the same space. Lovey finally turned the music down and turned around, drying her hands on the towel.

"Okay, lovebirds. I'm about to go upstairs and get myself decent while ya'll enjoy one another."

"Okay," Aries said as her scowl formed into a smile again. She watched as Lovey went over and placed her hand on Saint's shoulder, causing him to look up at her with a fake grin. Lovey walked over to Aries and did the same.

"Okay, baby. Don't be a stranger nah… you hear me?" Lovey said.

"Yes ma'am," Aries replied.

Saint watched closely as his grandmother exited the kitchen and disappeared upstairs. Just as she got out of eyesight, Saint lunged for the cereal box that was sitting on top of the refrigerator. Aries didn't move a bit. She just sat back in her chair, relaxed. She casually pulled the napkin from over her gun and grabbed it. She stood up as Saint's hand rummaged through the box.

"It's not dere'," Aries said. She had already searched the kitchen in the wee hours of the night and removed it.

"Who the fuck are you?" Saint asked, not believing how many steps ahead of him Aries was.

"A bitch yu' don't fuck with," Aries shot back. "Have a seat," she said calmly. Saint paused, took his hand out of the cereal box, and then he did as he was told.

"Just do what you going to do, love," Saint said smoothly.

"Me don't need permission. Me do have a few things to say though," Aries replied.

"I'm listening."

"Nigga, yu' got to," Aries reminded him and she gripped the gun even tighter.

"You right."

"You sent nigga to me shop. That's a no-no, yu' hear me? I don't play those type of games. Yu' can't force me to do shit me no want."

"Okay."

"Shut de' fuck up and listen," Aries shot back, slightly raising her voice, wanting Saint to understand her loud and clear. "Me don't bother anybody, so me want the same in return. Dis' is me town. Me run dis'. I run dis' town. Me not letting no man come and strongarm me. Just leave me alone and keep me out of your bullshit money schemes. Me cannot be extorted or forced to do anything me no want. Got it?"

Saint nodded in compliance. He looked directly at her with no fear, expecting a gunshot at any moment. Aries stood up and stared Saint down. She then grabbed a piece of pineapple and ate it.

"I love your grandma. She's a sweet lady," Aries said as she chewed the fruit. She smirked, knowing that she just sent an undertone threat his way. Saint watched as Aries walked out and onto the porch where Crow sat, looking towards the road.

"Yu' have a good day," Aries said as she stepped off the porch. Crow looked up in confusion as she walked off and down the street without a care in the world. A few seconds later, Saint stepped onto the porch seeing that Aries was far down the street. Crow was the first to speak.

"Morning brethren. Me didn't see her come in with yu'. Yu' snuck her in, eh? Yu' smashed?" Crow asked, thinking about how sexy Aries was.

"Nah... nah. Not yet," Saint said as he looked down at Crow in disgust. Saint thought about giving Crow a tongue lashing for letting someone creep up on him like that. However, he didn't want to admit that he had got caught slipping. He had to figure some shit out before he made any type of move. He still couldn't understand how she got past Crow. His mind was churning at that point. He was bothered and intrigued at the same time.

"Listen, I need you on the block holding shit down. You don't have to stand post no more, feel me?" Saint ordered as he tried his best to hold in his anger and disappointment.

Crow stood up and looked at Saint in puzzle-ment.

"Yu' sure?" he asked.

Saint just nodded his head up and down and went into the house, leaving Crow on the porch, boggled. Saint stepped in the house and put his hands on his waist as he looked around while shaking his head. As odd as it was, Aries had just turned him on. It was something about her that he liked. She was different. Aries was... well... she was Aries.

***

Sherriff Gipson was a slim, tall man who had a salt and pepper beard and a shiny bald head. He too was an island native so his skin resembled that. His golden-brown tone was a signature of most islanders. His nose was slightly bigger than normal and he had a friendly face. He sat at the desk with his feet crossed on top of it. He was in full uniform and a big gun rested in his holster on the belt line. He drank his morning coffee and was reading the local newspaper when the bell chimed.

Ding!

His attention went to the door and in walked Aries. He unfolded his feet and pulled his leg from the table. He smiled.

"Well, what do we have here? The queen of the island," he said jokingly. Aries walked to the desk and sat in the chair directly in front of him.

"Who the fuck is dis' new nigga?" Aries shot at him with a tone of irritation. Sherriff Gipson dropped his head with a slight grin.

"You're talking about the young guy that owns the teen club?" Sherriff Gipson said.

"Yu' know that's who me talking bout!" Aries spat.

"I don't really know too much about him. He came in a few months ago and bought the old jukebox spot and turned it into what you see now," Sherriff Gipson answered.

"What's his game?" Aries asked.

"Sweetheart, I don't get into that shit," he admitted.

"Is that right?" Aries asked skeptically.

"Yea. Just like half of this town. They come in for a while, clean up a bankroll, and then head out. You know how it goes. I just pick up my cut every month and turn the other way," he admitted.

"Okay, well, me no like him. Me need him to stay far away from me before I make things messy around here," Aries threatened.

"Aries..." Gipson said as he stood up, walked around the desk, and sat at the edge right in front of her. He continued. "You know I have a special relationship with you. I remember when your father and uncles ran this town. I saw you grow, leave, and then come back. I'll do whatever to help you. I'll take a look into it. Fair enough?" he asked.

"Yeah, okay," Aries said half-heartedly. She was so pissed that this out of towner had the balls to mess with her and didn't do his homework.

Although Aries was a fugitive back in the States, it was a known secret that the town was hiding her. The town took care of its own, but somehow Saint was able to slip through the cracks and violate the town's secret.

"You need to just let me handle this. You know you need to stay under the radar," Sherriff Gip said, referring to her being on the FBI's most wanted list for her past crimes. "Don't you worry about it. Just give me a few days and I'll get to the bottom of this."

"Okay, Gip," Aries said as she stood up and gave him a quick hug. Aries turned to walk out and just before she reached the door, Sherriff Gipson remembered something.

"Hey… one more thing," he said as he put one finger in the air.

"What time does Flower get to your shop in the mornings?" he asked.

"Me don't know… around ten most days. A few times she showed up early before sunrise but for de' most part around ten when me open."

"Okay, because she leaves here around eight every morning and I just want to make sure we look after her. You know them knuckleheads that be roaming around," Sherriff Gipson said, thinking about the strange tourists and local goons.

"Okay, I will." With that, Aries exited the precinct, leaving Sherriff Gipson there slightly concerned.

Chapter Five

A SHADE CALLED RED

Saint, Crow, and a middle-aged white man were inside The Wave. It was just after noon, so the place was empty and wasn't set to open until later that evening. They were in Saint's office handling business as they did every Saturday around the same time. The sounds of a money machine running filled the air, ending in a loud noise.

Beep!

Crow had just brought in a small grocery bag. It was full of money from the trap spots he ran for Saint. Meanwhile, Saint was at the table with his accountant who wore a well-tailored suit with big bi-focal glasses that rested on the end of his nose bridge. His skin was pale as snow and his hair was slicked back. He was a nerd, to say the least; a square. He punched a calculator as he took individual stacks of money from Saint as they came out of the machine. They had been doing that for the past hour or so. He neatly placed the stacks of bills side by side inside of the steel briefcase that sat open in front of him.

"That's all I can take this week," the accountant said as he stood up and buttoned one of his blazer's buttons. He reached into the inner pocket and pulled out a piece of paper. Saint looked at the check and shook his head.

"Fuck. It's going to take forever to run through that paper. We make this shit in a day sometimes." The accountant shook his head as if he was saying, *that's all we can do.*

He handed Saint a check for fifty thousand. In return, he would walk off with seventy-five thousand in cash. Saint loved that he could wash his money through a few anonymous investors, but he knew if he didn't figure this problem out, he would never be able to go legit. Or even worse, get the attention of the feds. He still had a nice amount of cash that he was sitting on. The amount of pills he sold to tourists was astronomical. He came from the school of cocaine but quickly learned that the party drugs did much better. They offered a friendlier clientele, rather than the street niggas he used to deal with in the States.

"Look, this is good money, but I must be honest with you. You need to find another source to run this money through. My investors are getting antsy, dude. It's only so much a teen club can make without tipping off the government. It's imperative to partner with a well-established hub. You need a business that's been up and running for a while. With heavy traffic AND cash transactions. If not, you're asking for trouble."

"I know… I know. I'm working on it," Saint said as he looked down at the check.

"Good," the man replied. Saint stuck out his hand for a shake and the accountant slid the briefcase off the table, shook Saint's hand, and headed towards the exit. Crow watched as the accountant exited and then focused his attention on Saint.

"Dat bitch from de' chicken spot not playing ball, eh?" Crow asked, referring to Aries.

"She different. I'll get through tho'… one way or another," Saint said, not even looking at Crow as he began to shove the remaining money on the table into an LV duffle bag. Saint loved a challenge and the fact that she was so stubborn and witty intrigued him. He was used to getting things his way, but with Aries, that wasn't the case. He looked at her as a challenge and that made her that much more interesting to him. Saint stood up with the bag in hand and looked at Crow.

"I need to holla at you too, my nigga," Saint said.

"What tis' it?" Crow asked.

"I know what you doing in my shit. Trust that," Saint said with certainty.

"What?" Crow said, playing dumb. Saint stepped closer to Crow, invading his personal space. Saint wanted him to hear what he was about to say loud and clear.

"Don't sell pills in my shit. I picked a teen club so we can stay under the radar. Not for you to get every teen on the island high off Xanax and Ecstasy."

Crow started to say something to explain himself, but Saint put his hand up, signaling him to shut the fuck up. Saint was visibly upset and it showed on his face. The muscles in his jaw were bulging and his chest began to rise. Saint clenched his teeth and began to speak again.

"Keep that shit on the block. No more trapping out the club. Do I make myself clear?" Saint asked. Crow paused and smirked.

"Yu' got it, boss man," Crow responded.

"That's right. I'm the boss. Remember that,"

Saint said as he headed towards the exit, leaving Crow standing there.

Saint made mental note to keep a close eye on his head lieutenant. He was getting too comfortable making decisions without letting him know. He wanted to nip it in the bud before it became a bigger problem later. Crow headed out and before he reached the exit, he yelled to Crow.

"I'll be through later in the morning to pick up that paper. Make sure that count right!" Saint yelled with no kindness in his voice.

"Got it, boss," Crow said sarcastically. And with that... he was gone.

***

Aries sat at the bar that was just a few steps from her house called Jimmy's. She would visit it sometimes because she liked the low-key setup. It had no cameras and didn't have any frills. It wasn't appealing to the eyes, so it wasn't very popular amongst tourists. They had good wine, decent vegan burgers, and was 420 friendly. All of which fared well with Aries. She sat there with her fat-stuffed joint and vibed out as Bob Marley pumped through the speakers. The ganja smoke was through the air and the doors were wide open to catch the summer breeze. Aries had an eventful day, so she wanted to end it on a good note. Trey was out with his friend, so she decided to unwind there.

As she took a pull of her joint, she noticed a girl kept looking in her direction. It was more than obvious that she had something that interested her in Aries' direction. Aries couldn't help but to notice and grow uncomfortable. It was a girl that Aries had never seen before. She had a head full of red hair and was done nicely. Her baby hairs that rested on her edges were even red, which went nice with her matching red lipstick and dark brown eyes. Her lips were big but in a good way. They were plump and appealing to the eye. Her skin was dark, smooth, and youthful. Her breasts were enormous and her plunging V-neck seemed like they barely were holding them up. Her pointy nipples peeked through her shirt and her titties bounced with each step. She had a nice ass, but not too big, just nice and round. The main event were them breasts though. They were a work of art and Aries couldn't help but stare. The smell of her sweet perfume made it to Aries before she did.

"Hey, I'll be serving you today. I'm Tammy, but everyone calls me Red," she said as she pointed at her nametag that read her nickname. She swiped across her melons, making sure Aries got another glance at them.

"Hey," Aries said simply as she focused back on Red's face. Red smiled, showing her nice white teeth.

"Can I get you... anything?" Red asked as she licked her lips and her face got serious. It was a look of seduction. Aries immediately felt her clitoris thump and it surprised her. She didn't swing that way but it was something about Red that gave her that unfamiliar sensation. Aries calmly crossed her legs, just to get that little friction on her button.

What the fuck? Aries thought as she gazed into Red's eyes.

"I'll take a Pinot Noire, please," Aries said just before she took a drag of her joint that was between her pointer and index finger.

"One Pinot Noire coming up," Red said before turning around and putting her bubble in front of Aries. She walked away and her wide hips swayed back and forth as she made her way around the bar. Aries watched her the whole way there. She took another drag and shook her head, grinning. *What the fuck is in this weed?* she thought to herself and chuckled.

"I'm tripping," she whispered under her breath. Red made her way back to Aries with a bottle of wine and a glass. She approached Aries with that same grin as she leaned over and sat the glass on the table.

"I gotta tell you. You are so pretty, girl," Red said as she flaunted her cleavage once again and poured Aries the glass of the wine.

"Aw... thanks. Yu' are too," Aries replied.

"Thank you! So can I eat anything?" Red said and instantly placed her hand over her mouth while her eyes grew big as golf balls.

"I am so sorry. Oh my God," Red said as she dropped her head and placed her hand on her forehead in embarrassment.

"Wow," Aries simply said as she looked away and put her tongue to her cheek. She had never been hit on by a girl.

"I meant... do you want anything to eat? On the menu of course," Red said as she pointed at the menu that was stuck in between the ketchup and mustard on the table.

"Nah, me good. Just de' wine is fine."

"Okay, well if you need anything else just let me know. I'll be here to check on you periodically. It's kind of slow tonight so... I'm all yours," Red said. She shook her head, knowing that she sounded thirsty again. "I can't catch a break tonight," she said. Aries laughed, easing the mood and causing Red to give a big smile as well.

"It's fine… it's fine. You're new around here, eh?" Aries asked.

"Yeah, I always wanted to live here after me and my ma traveled here on a cruise when I was a little girl. So, I looked for any job openings and just came," said Red.

"Just came, eh?" Aries added.

"Yeah, well that's until my writing career takes off."

"Oh, you're a writer?"

"Yeah, I've been writing all my life. I'm working on my first novel now."

"That's cool. What's it about?" Aries inquired.

"It's an island thriller about a serial killer and a relentless cop."

"Okay… okay. That sounds good. So, I guess you're going to be around a while for your research, eh?"

"I think so," Red answered as she ran her tongue across her top lip.

"I'll be seeing yu' around," Aries said as she put her joint in the ashtray and took a sip of the wine.

"I guess you will," Red answered as she walked off, leaving Aries sitting there with a wet ass. The chemistry was looming and Aries couldn't wait to get home to put her rose toy to work.

"Okay Miss Red," Aries said to herself as she

smirked and took another sip. She found her to be very, very interesting.

***

A row of dilapidated houses was on the long unpaved street. The ocean was still visible, but just out of earshot of the sounds of the crashing waves. This was the hidden slums of Bridgetown where only the locals and tourists looking for drugs or prostitutes went. This was the part of town that wasn't advertised on cruise ships' brochures or vlogs online.

Crow stood on the porch, carving small slices of a mango; his favorite fruit. He was shirtless and his body seemed to shine in the sun. Even though his skin was dark as charcoal, a gleam came off it. A small towel sat on his head as sweat formed just above his top lip and nose. He was watching the block do numbers. The teens and tourists were swarming. Pills were running rampant and they were the only true plug in a hundred-mile radius. They did wholesales and served direct. They were making a killing and Crow loved the fact that he didn't have to sleep on Saint's porch every night.

He felt resentment that Saint reduced him to a guard dog while he was his head lieutenant in his drug business. What he didn't realize was Saint had him close like that because he was the only one he truly trusted on the island. Saint and Crow were on opposite sides of the spectrum when dealing with feelings for one another. Then again, perspective was everythingespecially in street business. Many had lost their lives and wars have started simply because someone looked at a situation differently than their counterpart. Crow was ready to break loose from Saint, but he understood that Saint was the plug and he needed him. Saint never let Crow in on his source and that was a chess move on Saint's behalf. He understood the power of compartmentalizing the street business of iniquity.

Saint taught him about street logistics and how to run a block and it was showing. While Saint played the background, Crow was the face of their small drug enterprise.

"Yerrrr!" A hustler called out as a car went by and the young blonde driver ducked his head, looking for the address. The car stopped and the island boy ran to the car to take the order. Another came within twenty seconds later, so another island boy jumped off the porch to do the same.

Another Crow member sat in the windowsill of the trap house, looking over the street. He also had a speaker and pumped-out music by Burna Boy. Crow heard the song come on and stepped off the porch and looked up to the window.

"Turn de' sounds up." Crow swayed back and forth, making his hand in the shape of a gun.

Ye… Ye… Ye, Ye, Ye

Crow sang along and a few moments later, a group of island girls that were inside the trap came out. They heard the sounds of the latest of Burna Boy jam serenading the block.

> *My nigga, what's it gon' be?*
> *G-Wagon or de' Bentley?*
> *The gyaldem riding with me*
> *I no fit die for nothing*
> *My nigga, what's it gon' be?*

Three girls, all sexily dressed in minimal clothes. Their big asses hung out the bottom of their shorts with wide hips and heavy teardrop asses began to wine to the sounds, giving the men on the block something to look at. A few more Crows came out of the house and began to vibe as well. Everyone was in unison and had a rhythm that only an islander would; it was beautiful as they formed a circle. When the music stopped, people scattered around the trap and got back to the hustle.

There was a hand-to-hand transaction every two minutes and it was business as usual that afternoon. Bridgetown only had a few cops to run the island, so Crow's crew operated freely. He knew that they had bigger guns, better numbers, and more respect than the local authorities, so there was a small chance of getting caught. The trap only closed if the feds were in town. The island was known for money laundering because of all the offshore banks it had. It was over one hundred banks in the small town, so it was a drug dealer's dream to visit there. Some called it the 'Cleansing Capitol' of the Caribbeans. Drug usage and purchases on the island were as common as the retail stores by the dock. However, since the rise of crypto currency, the black-market business had slowed.

He watched as his soldier leaned into a car that had just pulled up. He quickly served a fiend and returned to the porch, joining Crow. He was husky and had a thick Cuban chain on, shirtless. His dreadlocks were unruly and thick. He was a prototype island boy. He went by the name Chubbs for obvious reasons. He held a small towel in his hand to wipe his sweaty forehead. He had a big tattoo across his chest that read M.O.C. As usual, the island was hot and muggy as the sun beamed down mercilessly.

"Chubbs, getting money today, eh?"

"All de' time!" Chubbs said as he slapped hands with Crow. He showed his gap tooth smile and Chubbs stood next to Crow on the porch.

"Yu' see all de' fat asses on de' block?" Chubbs asked as he stared at the girls that were talking a few yards away from them.

"Yeah, too bad dey' give yu' no pussy," Crow said, sending a few of the Crows into laughter. Crow looked back and laughed himself.

"Fuck ya'll," Chubbs said as he looked back at members of the crew.

Chubbs was the only one that had trouble with the ladies and it was a running joke amongst their circle. Even his money didn't translate to favorable pussy. His physical appearance was gross to all the island girls and he was every lady's last pick. He hated getting teased for it, but what could he do? He had to settle for the local prostitutes and bottom of the barrel girls that the island had to offer.

In the midst of the ghetto congregation, Flower walked aimlessly down the block. She held a bouquet of sunflowers in her hand and admired them while taking her stroll. She would always stop in front of the trap and just look, being extremely curious. That was until someone shooed her off before she made the block hot. Everyone was occupied in their own business to notice her coming; no one noticed her. No one except Chubbs. He stepped off the porch and walked down the block away from the house. He approached her, cutting her off her path and out of earshot of everyone.

"Hey... it's Flower, right?" Chubbs said, flashing his rugged smile. Flower just looked down, avoiding eye contact, and fidgeted. Chubbs continued. "Yeah, that's it... Flower. Yu's a pretty gyal," he said as he rubbed the back of his hand on her hair. Flower jumped and cringed at his touch, but she never looked up.

"Yu' been walking up and down de' streets all summer. Yu' see something over here yu' like?" Chubbs said as he put his thumb under his Cuban link chain and slightly raised it off his chest. Flower slowly raised her head and her eyes landed on Chubbs' bling. She slightly grinned, which caused Chubbs to do the same.

"Yeah... yu' like dat," he said, not being able to hold back his big smile. He looked Flower up and down and then licked his lips. He began thinking about how tight her love box was. He was almost sure she had never had sex before and that made manhood instantly get hard. He rubbed it through his pants and then looked around. He noticed everyone was tending to their own business and wasn't paying them any mind. He ran his thumb across the tip of his pole and felt the sensation of pleasure go up his spine. Flower was beautiful and he knew that he would never be able to get someone of that tier any other time, so his mind began to think about the possibilities.

"Hey, walk over here with me and I'll let yu' wear my chain, okay?" Chubbs said as he began to walk towards the abandoned house that was a few houses down from the trap.

"I'll let yu' wear me chain AND come hang out with us in the trap spot, okay?" Chubbs said, trying to say anything that might entice her. Flower's eyes filled with glee and she clapped her hands, wanting to finally be where the happy music came from.

***

Meanwhile, down the street, Saint pulled up in his silver S-Class Mercedes Benz. Everything seemed to stop when he pulled up and all eyes were on him. He quickly hopped out the car. His open linen shirt displayed his stomach bulge and tattooed midsection. He also had a bulge below that showed with every step he took. His endowment was on full display. He had on dark shades and a bucket hat that was pulled low, slightly above his eyes.

"Peace. You got that for me?" Saint asked as he approached Crow who stood on the porch.

"Yu' know it," Crow answered while rubbing his hands together.

He headed into the house, leading the way for Saint. The girls in the front yard stared and tried to give Saint the hint that he could have them and do what he pleased to them. They giggled loudly and one girl did a little twerk shaking her ass, making it jiggle a little. However, Saint never looked their way. He had no interest in the young girls, while they were lusting after the town's boss. Saint was the most sought-after man on the island, but he never gave any woman attention in the open. He liked to be under the radar because he understood that being a womanizer was detrimental to his whole being.

Saint stepped into the house and felt the instant gush of the air conditioning. Inside had no furniture, just a long table, and hard steel chairs. A few girls were counting pills using a butterknife type tool to avoid miscounting. They scraped the pills into different colored medicine bottles to distinguish the drug. Then, they screwed a top on them and placed them in a box, ready to be sold. There were a few piles of pills and everything from Adderall, Xanax, Percocet, and Extasy were being prepped.

Saint walked past them and followed Crow into the back room where a few of his crew members were shooting dice. Money was scattered on the floor and the sound of the bones bouncing on the floor along with banter filled the air. Saint kept his head low and walked right past them, not even wanting them to know he was there. He slid past them and headed up the stairs to the second floor. A big door was at the top of the stairs and Crow got to it and knocked.

"Open de' door, brethren," he said loudly as he knocked in a rhythmic pattern.

He paused for a few seconds and looked back at Saint, who was a few steps down from him. The sound of multiple locks being unlocked echoed through the corridor and a young man with a head full of small dreads answered the door. It was the same person who played the speaker from the window. He was in the room alone and was the only person authorized to be in there outside of Crow. The young boy looked to be no older than twelve; however, his eyes showed that he had been through more than his age warranted. He had a chipped tooth and very light hazel eyes. Crow gave him a special handshake and then Saint came in and gave a head nod to greet him. The youngster smiled and returned the nod, seeing the man he wanted to be like one day.

"Jupe! Grab dat for boss man," Crow said as he made his way to the closet and pulled out a black duffle bag. He threw it on the floor towards young Jupe, which was short for Jupiter. It was an odd name, but his mom was a junkie and she always would be high as Jupiter. So, when she got pregnant, that's what she named her son.

Saint watched as Jupe got on his knees and removed a floorboard. A stash of money was placed neatly under it within the hidden compartment. Jupe began to pull the money out and tossed the rubber banded bundles into the bag. Saint nodded his head, loving what he was seeing. It was something that he liked about Jupiter and he made a mental note of that. He also thought about a small problem they had with some islanders from the next town. They were trying to come sell near the docks and get some of that tourists' money. That was a no-no and it had to be addressed.

"Heard anything from them city boys?" Saint asked as he tapped Crow on the chest.

"Yeah, we touched they ass up few days when we caught em' on dock," Crow confirmed.

"All that is attention that we don't need. Why keep touching up the goons that Trel sends? We need to go see Trel and stop it altogether. Kill the head and the body will drop, not the other way around. Ya'll keep playing with them lil'niggas. They need pressure, you hear me?"

"Cool. One through ten?" Crow asked.

"Ten," Saint answered without hesitation. With that number given, he just put a hit on his competitor's head without even saying it.

Crow nodded his head, signaling that he understood what needed to be done.

Saint got the bag from Jupe and peeked in. He looked over at Crow, whose eyes were on the money as well. Saint could sense the jealousy in Crow and he knew that eventually, he would have to deal with it. But for now, they needed each other. Crow had the streets and Saint had the plug. They were good apart but together they had something of value. One plus one always equaled three... in the streets.

***

Chubbs looked down at Flower as he stood on the side of the vacant house just down the block from the trap spot. Flower was on her knees, directly in front of him. She had Chubbs' Cuban link around her neck. Chubbs had his pants pulled down and rubbed his dick through his boxers. He shook and stroked it, trying to get it to wake up as he breathed hard and stared at Flower's lips. He stuck his tongue out and flicked it up and down, imagining giving Flower oral.

"Yu' want to go inside of the party house, right?" he asked as he looked down at her big, beautiful eyes. She had a look of joy on her face as she played with the chain, smiling from ear to ear.

"Yeah, there that smile go. Yu' want to go in there bad, eh?" Chubbs said as she gently palmed the back of her head. Flower then nodded her head up and down, agreeing with him.

"Well, yu' gotta suck on it for me, eh? Just like your sucking your thumb. It's easy breezy, gyal," Chubbs said as he pulled out his short, fat pole. He was semi-erect and his leg began to shake in excitement. He pulled Flower's head to his mid-section and tried to line up his penis with her mouth, but she instantly turned, making him miss the mark.

"Come on, Flower. Don't be like that. I let yu' wear my chain… plus we gon' de' best friends after this," Chubbs pleaded. Flower kept her head turned away from his penis and shook her head no. Now, her smile had turned into worry.

***

Saint jumped into his car and tossed the duffle bag in his backseat. He checked his mirrors and then pulled out. Like always, he stayed on point, checking his surroundings and made sure no one was following him. As he pulled down the street, his eyes moved from left to right and in passing, he saw Flower on her knees. He frowned as he passed her and Chubbs on the side of the house. He instantly frowned and thought about what he just saw. He stopped the car and put it in reverse. He pulled into the driveway and Chubbs was so busy trying to get Flower to suck him up, he never saw Saint coming. Saint walked behind him just as he was getting aggressive with Flower, forcefully grabbing her hair, and jerking her around as he scolded her.

"Bitch, me tired of playing games witchu'. Yu' betta eat dis mu'fucka!" Chubbs yelled as his face was twisted up in rage. That's when Saint crept up behind him and hit him in the back of his head with his pistol that he had pulled out from the small of his back.

"Aghh!" Chubbs yelled as he fell to the ground with his ass out and dick in the dirt.

"Fuck you on, nigga? Is you crazy?" Saint said as he reached down and helped Flower up. Chubbs turned and looked at Saint as if he was seeing a ghost. Saint reached down and brushed off Flower's knees and gently put his hand on her shoulder and looked down at her.

"Are you okay?" he asked her, genuinely concerned.

Flower shook her head quickly up and down as she looked down and twiddled her fingers. Saint took a deep breath and shook his head in disgust. Just the thought of someone taking advantage of a mentally challenged woman enraged Saint. He focused his attention back on Chubbs as he held his head, trying to regain his composure. Saint's hit had him seeing double. Saint looked at Chubbs' as his penis was still out and erect. This only infuriated Saint even more. He kicked Chubbs in the face, making him fly onto his back and blackout. There he was, laid out with his business on display for everyone to see.

"Let me see, love," Saint said as he reached over to Flower and took the chain off that was around her neck. He threw it on top of Chubbs as he lay there in la la land. Saint put his arm around Flower and guided her to his passenger side and opened the door for her then guided her in. He couldn't believe what he just saw and he didn't even want to think about what would've happened if he hadn't of came when he did. He had to get her off the block and he knew exactly where to take her.

Chapter Six

LIE TO ME, KING

Aries had begun burning sage and rolling up her weed while sitting at the kitchen table. Trey sat across from her on his computer. He was trading stock in a mock-like software.

"What yu' got going over there?" Aries asked as she sparked her weed.

"Nothing much, just moving around some currency and playing in the market," Trey said as he typed without taking his eyes off the laptop screen.

"Yu' are so smart, boy. Do yu' know that?" Aries said as she stopped to look at her growing boy. It seemed like yesterday that he would jump into her lap and stay latched on to her. Now, those days were long gone and he was growing into a young man.

"Ma... come on. Don't patronize me," he said as he finally looked at her and smiled.

"Patronize yu,' eh? That's a big ass word. Don't lemme' find out you smelling yu' self. Yu' balls finally dropped?" Aries said as she leaned back and sparked her joint. She took a deep drag and turned her head to blow out the smoke away from Trey.

"Huh?" Trey said, not knowing what his mom was talking about.

"Nothing," Aries responded. She just sat back and stared at her son. That's when a thought came across her mind.

"Yu' get some pump um yet?" Aries asked with a half serious and half joking.

"Come on, Ma. You're making me uncomfortable," Trey said as he blushed and smiled.

"Yu' can tell me, yu' know? I'm here if yu' ever need to talk bout' it," Aries offered.

"Mom, you're being weird," Trey said as he shook his head from side to side and then focused back on his laptop.

"Weird me' ass. Make sure you strap that lil wiener up if yu' do get yu' some. Got that?" Aries instructed.

"Yeah, Ma. I know," Trey answered.

A knock at the back door startled Aries as her eyes shot to the rear of the kitchen where the back entrance was. Since Crow had come and fucked up her spot, she hadn't even gone back there to straighten things out. She wanted time to cool off because the sight of her place being trashed might've sent her to her old ways. She didn't want to do that so she decided to let it be for a few days and shut down the restaurant.

She put down her joint and stood up. A white man with a uniform was at the door with a clipboard in his hand. She approached the door and opened it.

"How may I help yu'?" she asked coldly, not expecting a package or visitors on that day.

"I have a delivery for Aries? The setup is done, I just need your signature here and we can head out," the man said as he held a pen up and presented a receipt and a piece of paper that needed to be signed.

"Setup?" Aries asked, confused about what the hell he was talking about. The man stepped to the side, exposing her back patio. Aries turned her head and a confused look grew on her face. She had brand new patio furniture, tables, and umbrellas, giving her spot an upgraded look. At first, she was puzzled, but when she thought about it, she smiled.

"Very smooth, Mr. Saint," she said under her

breath. She didn't want to admit it, but she loved the new look. Aries grabbed the pen and signed off under a fake name.

"Thank you," she said as she smiled at the delivery man and watched him walk away. His small crew followed him off the property and Aries walked around examining the new setup. She rubbed her finger over the expensive wood table and luxury style chairs and was impressed by the choice. Very tasteful.

"Ma!" Trey called from the kitchen. Aries looked back and headed back into the house. She stepped in and he was still focused on his laptop.

"Someone's at the door," he said casually. Aries walked past him and headed to see who was there. She had taught him to never answer the door because of her former life. She always said, *'yu' never know when de' devil will knock,'* so that was their rule. She approached the door and opened it. Who stood on the opposite side made her freeze.

It was Saint. He had Flower next to her, which baffled her. She looked at Flower as her head was down and she played with her fingers.

"What's dis' about?' Aries asked.

"I found her down bottom," Saint said, referring to the nickname of the trap.

"Down bottom? What she doing down there?'

Aries questioned.

"Shit… I don't know, love. I found her around some shit she shouldn't be. It's wolves down there, you know?" Saint responded.

"Come on, gyal." Aries said, not liking what she was hearing. She didn't want to hear anymore. "Go back there and pick some flowers for de' table, okay?" Aries said as she cupped Flower's face, forcing eye contact. Flower gazed at Aries briefly and then looked away as if she was ashamed. Flower nodded her head hastily and then headed inside of the house, leaving the two alone.

"Thank yu' for de' new tables," Aries said as she crossed her arms and leaned on the doorway.

"No problem," Saint said as he smiled and then ran his tongue over his damn near perfect teeth. "I figured it was the right thing to do."

"It was. It was smart," Aries said, thinking about what she contemplated on doing for her get back. Aries had a stern look on her face, making sure Saint understood that it was a passive threat rather than just small talk.

"Indeed. Just to let you know… I didn't call that shot. Shit wasn't supposed to be that aggressive. I just told the lil' nigga to come hassle you. Nothing physical."

"It's cool. Me know where yu' stay if it

happened again," Aries threatened.

"That's true. Aye, I gotta know. How did you get past my man at the door?"

"I have me ways."

"Come on, you gotta put me on game so I won't let the next nigga do it."

"Or bitch," Aries shot back.

"Damn," Saint said as he put both of his hands on his chest as if her words sent daggers through him. "I guess, I deserve that. I just want to say I apologize."

"I hear yu'."

Saint looked down at Aries' chest as her nipples showed through her sundress. He caught himself and looked back up into Aries' eyes. It was an awkward silence and Saint felt the tension so he decided to make amends.

"So, listen, I feel bad about what happened. Maybe I could take you out to make shit right. You know... for the bullshit that went down?" Saint asked. Aries wanted to immediately dismiss him and turn down his offer, but it was something about Saint that she was intrigued by. She looked at his beard and teeth combo and had to admit. *The nigga is fine as hell,* she thought to herself. She also thought about the fact that he looked out for

Flower. That alone made her soften up on him and consider. However, something in her wouldn't let her accept his offer.

"Nah, I'm good," Aries said as she shifted her weight to her other side and placed her hands on her hips. Saint just stared, admiring her natural beauty. He loved the way that she was beautiful without make-up or the extras. She was just her.

"I understand," he simply said and he dropped his head and rubbed his beard. "I guess, I'll see you around," he added as he stepped back towards the steps.

"Cool," Aries said. Saint turned around and walked off the porch. Aries watched him closely and loved the way he moved. He did everything slow. He took his time, always looking around and being aware of his surroundings.

"Aye," Aries called, causing Saint to turn around.

"I'll be at Jimmy's tonight around nine," Aries said, giving him a small smirk.

"A'ight bet," Saint said smoothly as he returned the grin. With that, he left and got into his car. Aries couldn't help but beam. It felt good to be hit on by a man. Aries returned inside the house to get to the bottom of the Flower situation.

***

Saint sat at the bar, sipping a glass of cognac as he played the back. Reggae played in the background and a few people were slow grinding on the dance floor. It was a good ambiance and people were having a good time. He looked over at Crow and a few goons across the room at the pool table area. They stayed out of the way but they were there to secure their boss and keep a close eye on him. Saint drank as he patiently waited for Aries to walk through the door. He looked down at his two-tone Rolex and saw that it was twenty minutes past nine.

"Damn, where you at, love?" he said to himself under his breath.

Ironically, Aries was walking in. Saint's eyes lit up when he saw her and her grace. He was surprised by what he saw. Aries wore a snug fitting dress and her hair was pulled up tightly in a neat bun, putting her soft baby hairs that rested on her edges on full display. Her dress was all-black with a hint of sheer in all the right places. It showed her curves like no one on the island had ever seen. She had a nice bubble that matched well with her slim, petite frame. It wasn't too much but it was just right for her size. Her heels made it sit up a little more than normal and Saint's eyes were stuck. She had a small clutch purse in hand, just big enough to fit her wallet, and a small caliber gun. She scanned the room and saw Saint at the back table. She smiled and walked over to him as he waited, greeting her with a smile.

"Hey," she said, smiling.

"Damn, ma. You're beautiful," he admitted. He reached for a chair and pulled it out for her. Aries sat and felt slightly uncomfortable. She wasn't used to wearing a dress. She hadn't dressed like that since she used to seduce men and eventually kill them for her previous job.

"Thanks," she said as she sat down then Saint pushed her chair in.

"What you drink?" Saint asked.

"I'll take a Pinot Noire," she answered.

"Bet. Got you," Saint said as he lifted his hand and looked towards the bar.

Red was working that night. Red noticed Saint and came from around the bar. Red wore a catsuit that hugged her body tightly with her fat camel toe print on display. Her lips were swollen and it was obvious that she was without panties. Her big, round titties were sticking straight forward and as usual, she had big red hair. It was curled and her glossy lips were red. Her oversized eyelashes highlighted her eyes and every time she walked across the floor, all eyes were on her.

She smiled when she noticed who was at the table with Saint. It was her crush, Aries. She walked right up to her and stared at her. Red was admiring her new look and licked her lips as she looked her up and down. Saint noticed the connection, looked at them both, and smiled at the two beautiful women in front of him, sizing each other up.

"Good evening," Red said as she placed the end of the pen in her mouth and sucked it a little.

"Hey, what's up? Red, right?" Aries asked as she couldn't help but look at her, the barbie. Her eyes couldn't help but see her fat pussy. She had wondered how it looked and now there was no guessing. It was fat. Just the thought made her button jump and she squirmed in her chair as she put on a smile to hide her lustful facial expression.

"Yeah, that's right," Red answered.

"Aries?" Red asked.

"Yeah, that's right." Aries couldn't remember if she had told Red her name before so she was confused. But then again, she did get high and that was the only downside to weed in Aries' eyes. She hated the way it fogged her short-term memory.

"Ok, a Pinot Noire," Red answered as she breathed hard as if she was getting hot and bothered by Aries. The attraction was more than obvious and Saint just watched, not believing what was unfolding right in front of him. He raised his glass to break up the love session. He cleared his throat and Red blinked her eyes as if she was snapping out of a trance like state. Red was looking at Aries all done up and made Aries more attractive. She looked at that bubble and thought about it being in her face. She squeezed her pussy muscles and it felt so good to her. Her pussy tightened and contracted, making it moist. She felt the juice leaking.

"Oh, I'm sorry. Would you like another glass?" she asked as she focused on Saint.

"Sure," he answered as he downed the drink, handing her the glass. She retrieved the glass and walked to the bar. But not before looking back at Aries, making sure her eyes were where they were supposed to be; on her ass.

"Damn, she on you," Saint said as he noticed the flirting.

"Me don't swing that way," Aries said as she turned to look at Saint.

"Hey, I'm not judging," Saint countered as he held up his hands. Aries looked back at Red and shook her head.

"Anyways. How yu' feeling tonight?"

"I'm smooth. I appreciate you coming to have a

drink with me. This a cool spot too."

"Yeah, it's low key and has good vibes."

"Just like you," Saint said as he smirked. Aries pushed her cheek with her tongue and couldn't help but to smile at his witty response.

"So, what's your deal? Why yu' ask me out dis' week, but last week yu' sent nigga to de' house?" Aries asked, being blunt with him.

"Look, I was serious when I told you that wasn't my call. That nigga, Crow, a hothead," Saint said as he looked over to the area where he was. Aries' eyes followed and then she focused back on Saint.

"Yeah, me hear yu.' But you gotta to know next time yu' send him, I'mma send em back in a box."

"Yo, who are you?"

"What yu' mean?"

"Regular females don't talk like you. They don't move like you. It's just… it's different.

"Well, me not dese otha' bitches," Aries spat back, smirking.

"I see…" Saint said as he looked around then leaned in close. "I know who you are," he admitted. After a small pause and a few seconds of staring and quietness, he continued.

"Murda Mama," he whispered. Aries' heart dropped to her stomach as the words came out of his mouth. "I heard you and your team didn't fuck around. Damn near like a myth. Everybody knows about the Cartel family… that shit documented. And if you dig deeper, ya'll was tied to that. Ya'll legends back home. They got fifty documentaries on ya'll crew on YouTube. It wasn't hard to find after digging."

"What yu' want from me?" Aries said, cutting to the chase, understanding that he knew more about her than she was comfortable with.

"Shit, I don't need anything from you. To be honest, it just made me more intrigued. You a bad girl… a gangster," Saint said as he sat back while studying Aries.

"That was me old life. That's why me came back home, away from de' madness. That's something that me want to put behind me and let it stay there. That life is dead."

"Fo sho… I won't disturb that. I see what you doin.' I just wanted to know who I was dealing with while I'm doing my thing."

"And what is your thing exactly?" Aries asked, already partially knowing the answer.

"You turning into a ghost," Saint said frankly. Aries nodded her head, knowing that Saint had understood the rules of an endgame. Becoming ghost was a term that old hustlers used as a pathway to street retirement.

"And if a nigga get in de' way of that it can get spooky," Aries threatened.

"Listen, I get it. I'm doing my own shit, to be honest, and I don't need any unwanted attention in this town whatsoever," Saint stated.

"Well, it looks like we on de' same type of time," Aries said.

"The streets talk. I called back home and they gave me your credit report," Saint added.

"Then yu' know," Aries said as she ran a finger over her double M tattoo that was on her hand. Saint nodded his head, agreeing. Red returned with Aries' glass.

"Buy two… get one free. It's a threesome," Red said as she looked at Saint and then at Aries.

"You got something on your mind?" Saint asked, getting the hint.

"No, why would you say that?"

"Thank yu' for de' drink," Aries interrupted, growing irritated with the whole situation.

Red sensed the tension and walked off with a smile. Aries had to admit; Red was sexy and if she did do something with a woman it would be her. Red was super aggressive and that threw Aries off and threw up red flags. She wanted her too bad… but why?

"So, what's your plan in life? What is the

perfect situation for you?" Saint asked, trying to learn more about the woman across from him.

"To be honest, me living me dreams. Me always wanted to come back home and live amongst me people. No drama… no attachments. Just a free mind," Aries answered.

"What about love?" Saint asked, not expecting that answer from her.

"Love will get yu' killed. Love will have yu' doing shit that yu' normally wouldn't do. And if yu' talking about sex, me a big girl. Me know how to get myself off very well. And I got a rose that works wonders," Aries said, more serious than a heart attack. Saint nodded his head, taking in all that she was saying. It was a mouth full. Aries looked over at Saint's crew and then at Saint.

"Yo, let's get out of here. You can leave without your flunkies, right? Or yu' scared?" Aries said, feeling uncomfortable with Crow looking over at her repeatedly. She didn't like him and didn't want to be anywhere around him. Also, she always wanted to be the looming presence… not the other way around. Saint followed Aries' eyes and already knew what time she was on. He respected the move and it only added to the mystique of this gamed-up island girl sitting across from him.

"That ain't a problem. We out, love," Saint said as he dug into his pocket and placed a hundred-dollar bill on the table. He stood up and left for the door discreetly and Aries waited a few seconds and followed him. It was as if they were running away from authorities the way they slipped out without being noticed. They both got outside and giggled, looking back into the bar, seeing Crow and the others playing pool and not looking at them at all.

"Come on. I parked in the back," Saint said as he walked around the bar and towards the rear. Saint walked towards his truck while looking back at Aries. Aries took one look at the truck and grinned. She was impressed. It was a powder blue, old-school pick-up truck in mint condition. 84' to be exact and she knew that off first glance.

"This yu'?" she asked as he walked over to the passenger side and opened the door for her.

"Yea. Not too flashy but she gets the job done," Saint said modestly as he dropped his head and smirked. Aries stopped at the rear of the truck and ran her hand across the top of the back gate, feeling the heavy metal. She loved the way cars were made back in the day. Everything was solid and heavy… just like she liked her circle.

"84' right?" Aries asked, already knowing the answer. Saint tilted his head and squinted his eye. He was impressed.

"Yeah, that's right. How you know that?" he asked.

"Me poppa had one dese. He used to let me ride in de' back when he made his way around town. Me used to love catching the breeze. Especially at night."

"In the back?" Saint said as he eyed the bed of his truck.

"Yep, just me and him. He would even let me hit de' ganja a few times," Aries said just before letting out a giggle, thinking back at the good times she shared with him. Saint pulled out his phone and shot a text as he closed his door and walked up to her. He hovered over her and Aries could smell the light scented cologne coming off his body. She closed her eyes and took a deep breath, loving the aroma. It was nothing like a good smelling man. Saint stared down at her in admiration. He reached around her and unlatched the truck's gate, bringing it down. Aries stepped back and tried to see what he was doing.

"Yo!" Saint called out as one of Crow's goons was coming out with a bottle of wine in his hand. As he walked up, he handed the bottle to Saint.

"Slowly… around the island," he simply said as he tossed the goon the keys.

The goon caught the keys and headed to the driver's side. He hopped in and started the engine, causing the loud torque sound to fill the air. Although it was an older truck, it was powerful. Saint walked to the back of the truck and hopped up to have a seat. The bottle was still in his hand. He looked at Aries and raised the bottle.

"Can you please join me for a late ride around the island?" Saint asked while looking at her.

"Very smooth, sir. Very smooth. Me would love to," Aries said as she held her hand out and waited for Saint to help her up and onto the truck bed. She got in and they both sat with backs to the driver as they pulled off slowly and hit the road.

They cruised on the edge of the island and near the boardwalk, so the sounds of the ocean were loud, thudding, and calming at the same time. The waves seemed to crash a little louder that evening, so it acted as their night's soundtrack as they took turns drinking wine directly out of the bottle. It seemed like the beginning of a special night.

Chapter Seven

SEA OF RED

Jalen and Trey were on the steps of the trap house. Most of his brother's crew were in the city with Saint, so Jalen took that as an opportunity to hang out there. Jupe sat in the second-story window, half of his body hanging out as usual. He oversaw the block and watched the people below.

"I can't believe your mom let cho ass stay out this late," Jalen said as he drank a beer. Trey had one in his hand too but he had barely touched it. They had been sitting there for the past hour, admiring the girls walking up and down the street half naked trying to sell pussy.

"Aw baby, show me a titty," Jalen called as one of the curvy women with a sheer dress walked past. She had on stiletto boots and everything was on full display. You could see her entire body with what she had on.

"Give me some money and I'll let yu' do more than see it. I'll put that fat ass pussy on yu' too," she said as she continued to talk with her group of girls. The others laughed, knowing that the young guys wouldn't know what to do if they even got a chance to smell it. Only one streetlamp worked so the working girls were in the shadows, hoping to catch a john to turn a trick. Just like clockwork, two cars pulled up back to back and like moths to a flame, the women flocked to the vehicle trying to get chose.

"That's crazy how them dudes pay to sleep with girls. And that's after they been sleeping with other multiple men all day. Yuck. I don't get that part."

"That's the game, bro. You gotta get hip. Pussy is hot commodity around these parts," Jalen stated.

"Who would want that? Seems nasty as hell."

"Pussy a make nasty shit seem okay. You know how that wet feel," Jalen said as he took a swig of the beer and playfully nudged Trey as he reminisced about how it felt. Trey started to blush red and had a look of embarrassment on his face. Jalen instantly picked up on Trey's uncomfortableness.

"Wait mu'fucka. I know that look." Jalen stood up and looked intensely at Trey. He smiled when the thought came into his mind. It was obvious as day. "You never got no pussy You're a fucking virgin, ain't you?" he asked.

"Man, chill out," Trey said, trying to brush off the subject.

"Nah nigga. Ain't no chill. You here with the desert dick," Jalen said just before bursting out in laughter at his own joke. "Wait here," Jalen instructed as he put a finger up.

He took a quick swig of the beer and then headed into the house; Trey stood outside alone. Well, just him and the whores who walked past him every few seconds. He was admiring the fat, jiggly asses, and big breast that were on full display for anyone who would look in their direction.

That's when Trey realized that he was dealing with the heavyweights of the town. These were the ones that didn't come out until night. Their asses were humongous and bodies were amazing. Some were surgically enhanced while others were natural. However, they were ghetto street stars and extremely sexualized. Trey just watched closely as girls jumped in cars, talked inside of cars, and shook their asses, giving themselves a small commercial for the potential johns.

Moments later, Jalen returned from the inside of the house, but this time he had one of the older homies with him. The tall, dark Crow member walked past Trey on the porch and whistled at the group of girls that were on the street.

"Sparkle!" he yelled out, making one girl step closer to see what he wanted. It was her… Sparkle. She was short, thick, and chocolate. She had low cut jean shorts that made her ass cheeks hang out the back of them. She had a bathing suit bra that could barely hold her triple D breast in place. She looked at the man and smiled, showing her gap-toothed smile. Her lips were oversized, textured, and glossy. Her bright, lime green lipstick gave her an extravagant look. Her big eyelashes fluttered with every blink and she was headed directly to them.

"Hey daddy," she said as she approached the tall Crow member.

He leaned in and whispered something to her. She listened for a second and leaned over to look around his body. She focused on Trey; who sat on the porch, trying to pretend that he wasn't paying attention, but he was. He was trying to see what was going on. She looked back at the man as if she was disagreeing with something. She was shaking her head no, but after the man leaned down and whispered something else to her, she stopped. Her demeanor changed. Her hand was now on her hip and she used the other one to show the symbol of money. She rubbed her thumb and index finger together as she loudly popped the bubble gum in her mouth. He must've told her what she wanted to hear because her attention left from o him and turned to Trey. Trey could feel the girl staring at him.

Oh shit, he thought as he swallowed hard and looked at her voluptuous shape. She was now heading directly to him as she swayed her hips from side to side with each step. She was swinging that ass from New York to Cali, coast to coast as she swayed. She wanted Trey to see what was on the menu.

"Yu' big man on island, eh?" Sparkle said as she approached Trey and put her hand on his chest. Trey was stuck and didn't know what to say. He looked down at her manicured hand and saw her extraordinary nails that matched her lipstick color.

"Huh?" Trey replied, not knowing what to say exactly. He had never had a grown woman give him that energy before. Jalen watched and snickered under his breath as the nervousness was all over his man's face.

"Yu' heard me, big mon," Sparkled said as she dropped one of her hands and placed it over his crotch, then squeezing it gently. Trey flinched but at the same time felt that tingle. He liked it and his body gave an immediate reaction. Sparkled looked down and smiled, seeing him get excited.

"There he goes. Big mon for sure," she said as she ran her tongue over her top lip and looked into Trey's eyes seductively. She grabbed him by his beltline and pulled him into the trap. She led the way as Trey's eyes followed her ass going into the spot.

"Boom! Boom! Boom!" Jalen yelled as he made finger guns and pretended to shoot them into the air. The few hustlers outside on the porch yelled out, encouraging Trey to become a man. Trey couldn't help but to smile as he looked back at the hooting and hollering.

***

"So, why would yu' be untruthful to your lady?" Aries asked in response to a deep conversation they were having. She had loosened up because of the wine and was enjoying herself. The ganja had her relaxed as well.

"I just wouldn't. You asked me what is my ideal relationship, right? I'm telling you that at my age, I would never get into a position that I would have to lie to my lady. I wanna be able to always keep it real. The good, bad, and ugly. Understand?" Saint said as he passed her back the joint. The truck slightly rocked as the road conditions gave them a satisfying vibration.

"That's de' problem. Niggas lie to de' world, making them happy, yu' know? But dey' come home and give woman all de' pain and weight of de' world," Aries said before she paused and took a deep drag of the weed. She looked up directly at the sky and exhaled the smoke.

"Shit… lie to me. Put on de' mask and make me feel that ever ting is okay."

"Damn," Saint said under his breath as the weight of what she said hit him. Aries looked at him and saw his mind taking in what she was saying.

"Black women get crowned for being strong and resilient. But sometimes, me want to feel vulnerable. Sometime me want to be a sheep and not de' wolf that de' world forces me to be. True femineity is happiness," Aries said as she passed the joint back to Saint.

Saint let what she said live in the space between them. It was poignant, so he gave it its proper due of silence. At that moment, Aries began to like Saint. She knew that he understood what she had just said and instead of giving an answer or rebuttal, he absorbed it. That was because Saint understood the art of allure. Words were the key. Not the words that a person may say, but the words that a person keeps. The art of listening versus talking was rarer than most realized. Saint understood that a woman wanted to be heard, so he did just that. The art of listening with the intent of understanding more so than replying was charming... no, it was gangster. Aries loved gangsters.

"So... what's your story? Obviously, me know why yu' came to de' island. But where did yu' come from?" Aries asked.

"I'm from everywhere. I moved around a lot," Saint answered smoothly.

"Everywhere, eh? Why yu' so secretive? Yu' a cop," Aries said jokingly. Saint chuckled at her remark.

"Definitely ain't a mu'fucka cop, love."

"Me get it. Yu' don't expose too much. Me know your type."

"My type? What's that?"

"Quiet money."

Saint nodded his head and smiled. "You want to know about me. How about you? Where you from?" Saint shot back. Aries smiled.

"Everywhere," she replied. They both burst into laughter and instantly understood that they were cut from the same cloth.

***

"Just relax," Sparkle said as she felt Trey's tension and nervousness. His body was as stiff as a board as she kneeled in front of him. She had his super erect penis in her hands as he looked down at her with sweat beads on his nose and forehead.

"I'm sorry," Trey said in a shaky voice.

"You never had head before?" Sparkle asked while already knowing the answer. Trey quickly shook his head from side to side, being honest about his inexperience. He squeezed his butt cheeks as hard as he'd ever done. He could crack a walnut between those two.

"Okay, well just sit back and relax. I got you," Sparkle advised as she placed one hand on his chest and gently pushed him back onto the couch even more. Trey stared at the ceiling and waited for the sensation that he had thought about daily. He was too nervous to even look down. He then felt big, wet lips wrap around his penis, which made him flinch in pleasure. She began to go up and down on him, wrapping her tongue around his pole with each bop. Trey moaned involuntarily as she gave him head. His pole was so hard that it hurt. As she went to work and the more Trey thought about what was happening, it was a recipe for disaster.

"Ohhh shit!" Trey yelled. He felt a climax

approaching and then Sparkle gave him a final slurp and hand yank. That was the end of that. He exploded on her face and nearly covered her face. His body went limp and involuntarily jerked as he experienced his first blow job orgasm. Sparkle stood up, wiped her mouth, and straightened out her clothes.

"Go clean ya' self-up, daddy," she said. "Welcome to manhood."

***

Crow and a few of his men approached the truck, just coming back from Jimmy's. Crow got impatient with Saint and got tired of waiting at the bar for them. He wasn't answering his phone, so he just left and returned to the block. That same moment, Trey was walking out with Sparkle to a wave of claps and cheers. Crow looked around and wondered what was going on.

"What's de' noise for, eh?" Crow asked as he looked at Jalen, who was leading the banter.

"My man right here, just got his knob shined," Jalen said proudly as he threw an arm around Trey's neck excitedly.

"Ohhh. Sparkle taste dem, eh?" Crow said as he watched Sparkle sway her big ass as she stepped off the porch. She gave Crow a seductive look as she wiped off her mouth. Crow turned to follow her ass and then turned back to focus on Trey.

Trey had been side-eyeing him since the day he trashed his mom's spot, so Crow saw that as an opportunity to clear the air. He knew that Trey could be valuable to him with his savviness with tech. He walked up to him and smiled, showing those infamous permanent, shiny, gold teeth that were laced with diamonds.

"Me know yu' don't like me," Crow said, referring to the obvious.

"It's cool, man," he said nonchalantly. He avoided eye contact with Crow because of his intimidating look. Trey was forgiving by nature and his mom taught him to not hold grudges. Trey's heart was pure; his good nature and naivety was obvious.

"Good." Crow went into his pocket and pulled out a wad of money. He peeled off five hundred one dollars bills and handed it to Trey. Trey's eyes lit up and he accepted the cash, hesitantly stuffing it into his pocket.

"Where mine, big bro?" Jalen said jokingly, but deep inside he was serious. Crow never gave him cash and always dismissed him as a brother. Before their parents died, Crow always felt Jalen was treated differently because of his parents' disdain of his physical appearance.

"Yu' put in de' work… you get money," Crow shot back with a smug look. A few of Crow's goons laughed because Jalen had a salty look on his face. Jalen frowned up and shrugged his shoulders.

"Man, let's go," Jalen said as he glanced at Trey and brushed past the few goons. Trey followed closely behind and they headed back towards the shore. Trey wanted to make it back before his mom did. However, this time it would be different when he entered his home. He would be walking in… a man.

***

"That was cool. Me appreciate de' ride," Aries said as they sat on the open gate of the trunk. They had been passing the joint back and forth for the past half an hour. It seemed as if they talked about everything that night. They seemed as if they had opposite viewpoints on most things, but that made for great intimate conversations by arguing their respective sides. They both were mentally stimulated and high as a motherfucker in the process.

"Yeah, I had a good time," Saint said as he eyed the bar's rear. His attention was off as he saw Red, who kept looking at them. Her attention was off as she was aware of her surroundings.

"Why you keep looking over there?" Saint said as she followed her eyes.

"Just checking de' ol' gyal from the bar. She keeps looking over here," she said as she noticed Red from afar. She was sitting on the back stairwell smoking a cigarette.

"You be on point, huh?" Saint said as he respected the way she moved and thought. She was careful like he was and Saint was overly impressed. It seemed the more he was in her presence, the more he was intrigued by her.

"Bitch, acting federal," Aries said as she squinted her eyes, trying to organize her thoughts.

"Nah, I just think she got a crush on you, love. You see how she was on you at the bar. She want you fa' sho," Saint said, smiling as he glanced at Aries.

"I don't swing dat' way," Aries corrected him.

Saint used that as an entryway to ask deeper questions. They had talked about everything that night so he felt it was a good time.

"You never even thought about it?"

"Thought about what?"

"You know... being with a woman."

Aries paused and blew out the weed smoke. It seemed as if she really thought about her answer before she gave it to Saint.

"I mean... me dreamed about it before," Aries admitted.

"One time, huh?" Saint said as he side-eyed her and lifted his head like he didn't believe her.

"Yu's a nosy mu'fucka, eh?" Aries said as she smiled and took a pull of the joint and looked at it and then at him. "Well, maybe three or four times."

They both burst out into laughter. Aries began to choke on the weed smoke as she held her fist to her mouth with one hand and her hand on her chest with the other. She passed it over to Saint as they both were tickled.

Saint looked at his watch and knew that he had to leave.

"Yo... I have to shake. Gotta give Lovey her medicine before she forgets," Saint said.

Aries nodded her head. She admired the way he looked after his grandma. Saint was a gangster but it was nothing more gangster than looking out for your family. Aries respected that more than anything or any amount of money he could show her.

"That's cool. Me had a great night. Haven't had that much fun in a very long time," Aries said.

"I enjoyed myself too. Thank you for riding out with me, love. Hopefully, we can do it again," Saint said as he stood up off the truck and stood in front of her. Aries looked up at him, while still sitting down and smiled. He stepped closer to her and she inhaled deeply, smelling his clean scented cologne. Saint stared down at her and her full lips. He slowly leaned down, going for a kiss.

Damn dis nigga smell good, she thought as she placed her hand on his chest, preventing him from stepping any closer. Saint paused, feeling he overstepped his boundaries.

"Have a goodnight, Mr. Saint," Aries said, giving him a sly grin.

"Cool. You have one as well," Saint said as he held out his fist, giving her a fist bump.

"Let me take you home," he said.

"Nah, me good. I'mma big gyal," Aries said as she stood up and straightened up her dress.

"Come on, it's getting late. Let me at least do that, so I won't worry," Saint pleaded. He stepped back and gave his goon a nod to step out of the car.

"I'mma walk. I literally live two doors down," Aries said strictly, giving Saint a hint to back off.

"Ok... ok," Saint said as he threw up his hands as if he was waving his white flag. Aries walked away and Saint watched her slim, thick figure cross the parking lot and in the bar's direction. He jumped into the truck and his goon pulled off.

Aries approached the bar and just as she was about to turn the corner, heading towards the front, she heard someone call her name.

"Hey, Aries!"

It was Red. She was still sitting on the stairwell and had just finished her cigarette. Red slid a piece of gum into her mouth and stood up. Aries stopped in her tracks. She put her focus on Red as she approached her—walking slowly, rocking those big hips and backside with each step.

"Had a hot date, huh?" Red said, trying to start small talk.

"Something like that," Aries said nonchalantly. Red slid her hands into her back pockets, putting her slim waist on display.

"So… come on. Tell me about it, girl," Red said as she gave Aries the biggest smile ever.

"It's nothing to talk about really. We just went for a ride," Aries replied. Aries just stared at Red for a second and had to admit to herself; Red was drop dead gorgeous. She was skeptical about her because she seemed aggressive, trying to force some type of friendship and that was against everything Aries believed in. She didn't like friendly bitches and never trusted women outside of her crew in her former life. She couldn't get a read on Red and that kind of scared her. Red noticed that Aries was in deep thought and she returned the gaze. She looked at Aries' lips and then her eyes drifted to her small, perky breast and then down to her hips. She wanted Aries and she couldn't hide it. Red's preference was women; her shape and good looks had afforded her the luxury of seduction.

"A ride? Was it bumpy?" Red asked as she stepped closer to Aries. Aries didn't say anything as Red stepped closer, invading her personal space.

"Did your pussy jump?" Red asked as she was now face-to-face with Aries.

She was so close; their noses were damn near touching. Aries wanted to step back or tell Red not to get so close, but she couldn't. She was curious and it was killing her cat. Aries felt the pulsing sensation down below and the feeling of shame overcame her. She knew that she shouldn't be feeling the way she was now. But between the weed, the night's cool breeze, and Red's juicy lips... Aries was hypnotized. Red leaned in and lightly kissed Aries' lips. Aries was hesitant, but she kissed back. Red's soft lips felt so good against hers and she had never felt anything like it. There was something about a woman's lips that was different from a man's and Aries learned that at first touch.

Red's lips were like soft clouds and Aries opened her mouth slightly. Red turned her head to the side and slipped her tongue inside Aries' mouth. Red began to circle Aries' tongue with hers and kissed her softly in between rotations. Aries kissed her back and then grabbed her around the neck while doing so.

Red reached down and slightly lifted the front of Aries' dress. Red dipped her hand into Aries' panties and moaned when she felt her wetness. Red took her two fingers and lightly rubbed them across Aries' clitoris. Her clitoris was slightly erect and peeking out of her vaginal lips.

"Wait... what de' fuck yu' doing?" Aries asked as she closed her eyes and grabbed Red's arm.

"I'm setting you free. I'm sorry, but I want you so bad. So bad..." Red admitted in an exasperated whisper.

Red applied more pressure to Aries' clit and pressed it while circling her love button. She slightly raised the intensity and the sounds of Aries' wetness made noises. The fact that they were in public behind the building, made the experience that more intriguing. The voyeurism made aroused them. Red gently pushed Aries' back against the brick wall. Aries felt the rugged concrete on her back as she closed her eyes and moved her hips, grinding against Red's fingers. Red slowly dropped to her knees and Aries panted as she watched her go down. Red reached into her pants and began to pop herself. She reached up and pulled Aries' panties to the side, making her love box plump out. Red loved the swollen look and couldn't contain herself. She began to tongue kiss Aries down below. Red slowly bopped her head back and forth as she tightened her lips over Aries' clitoris. She made her lips tight like a tight vagina. Red made Aries' erect clit plunge in and out of her tightened lips. Red moaned with each thrust.

"Oh me God," Aries said, as she began to grind her pelvic area in Red's face.

Aries placed her hand on the back of Red's head and sped up her mid-section plunges. Aries threw her head back in pleasure and then looked down at Red as she pleased her. Aries alternated between looking at the sky and down at Red.

The sky... and then Red.

Sky... Red.

Sky... Red.

"I'm about to cum! Oh... oh me God. Keep sucking. Right there. Suck it hard!" Aries instructed Red, who was now going crazy on her.

A few seconds later, Aries climaxed, wetting Red's entire face with her honey. Aries leaned her head against the brick wall and panted heavily as she pushed Red's head away. She then pulled down her dress and took a few deep breaths with her eyes closed, trying to regain her composure and stop her legs from shaking. She couldn't believe what just happened. She couldn't believe what she did. She could only think, what would her girl, Miamor, think. She could hear Miamor's voice in her head. *Bitch… no you didn't.*

Without saying a word, Aries straightened up her dress and watched as Red stood up with her hands still in her own panties, steady playing. Aries didn't know what she was looking at her for… she was done. Aries gained her composure, pulled her shoulders back, and walked off. It was time for her to go home.

"What a fucking night," she said under her breath as she turned the corner, leaving Red there alone.

***

Saint couldn't believe what he just witnessed. He was smiling and shaking his head as he watched the show. Red looked directly over to him and smiled as she straightened her clothes and wiped her mouth off. Saint was stuck. He made his goon creep back, just so he could make sure Aries got home safely. Although she refused, the gentleman in him couldn't let her do that at night. However, on his circle back, he got a voyeur show and he was shocked but happy that he got to witness the two savages behind the building.

Chapter Eight

MEETING WITH THE DEVIL

Aries could smell the scent of Red's perfume on her as she approached her door. She was still wet in between her legs and she couldn't wait to get into a hot shower. The thought of Red's mouth and tongue made her clit pulsate. The sensation demanded an involuntary pause and gasp, causing Aries to stop in her tracks and lean against the pillar on her front porch. It was in the wee hours of the night and she knew Trey was asleep. She didn't want to wake him, let alone let him know that she was coming in at the crack of dawn.

She carefully slid her key into the door and unlocked it. Once she entered, she instantly began to pull off her clothes so she could wash the sex off her. As she began to walk to the stairs leading to her bedroom, she smelled smoke. Her senses were immediately perked and she thought of her son and a fire. She looked up the stairs and then glanced around the first floor. She saw a small circle of fire coming from the direction of her sofa. She squinted her eyes and saw that a silhouette of a man was sitting on the couch. Aries instantly reached for her gun in her purse and pointed at the figure.

"Who's dere'?" Aries said in a calm voice, just loud enough for her intruder to hear.

She placed her finger on the trigger and slowly walked towards the lamp on the stand just to the right of her. She never took her eyes off the figure as she saw the ring of fire from the tip of the cigar brighten. The smoke danced in the air as Aries' eyes adjusted to the darkness. She now saw the Latino man in a white linen suit. Aries, still pointing the gun, reached over and turned on the light. She could clearly see the man's face and she squinted her eyes trying to figure out who was the mysterious man. She couldn't identify him and realized it was a new face. The man had a full salt and pepper beard and seemed to be in his early sixties. His olive-colored skin and textured hair hinted that he was of Latino descent. His hair was slicked back neatly. A cane rested against the couch and his legs were crossed as he continued to smoke the cigar without a care in the world.

"Good morning, dear," the man with the raspy voice said as he put out his cigar on the side table. The fact that Aries had a gun pointed at him didn't seem to bother him one bit.

"Who de' fuck are yu' and why are yu' in me fucking home, eh?" Aries asked as she looked at him with a piercing stare.

Aries inched her way closer to the man, pointing her gun directly at his forehead. She squinted one eye and had the precise aim that was needed to end him with one shot. But then he spoke as he slowly put his hands up with a smirk on his face. He had a smirk on his face as if a gun wasn't pointed at him. Aries' steady hand showed that there was no fear in her being. One false move and homeboy's brains would be splattered on the back wall.

"Please, let me introduce myself. I understand that this isn't the most charming way to meet for the first time," he said, moving his hands as he spoke. Aries stayed on him, finger on the trigger.

"Excuse, my friends behind you, they are there out of pure necessity." The mysterious intruder stood up and buttoned his blazer. He was smooth and had a welcoming smile on his face.

"What de' fuck do yu' want?" Aries questioned.

"Relax. If I wanted to kill you, you would

already be dead. I would've had my friends over here, blow out your brains earlier. I must admit, you put on quite a show on the beach."

Aries remained quiet and focused, ready to play it how it goes. The man walked closer to her and calmly slid his hands in his pocket, letting her know that he wasn't an immediate threat.

"My name is George Diaz. I came here to kill you and your son," he said and then paused, letting what he said sink in. Aries instantly shifted her stance, thinking about the safety of her son. She wondered if they had gone up the stairs already.

"If yu' lay a hand on me son—" Aries said but was cut off by Diaz.

"Relax, he's upstairs sleeping like a baby," Diaz replied.

"So, what chu here for?" Aries said, with an even heavier accent. She tended to do that when she was angry.

"Well, to be frank. If I wanted him dead, he would be just that. You see, your son took something from me."

"Bullshit. Chu have de' wrong person. My son isn't a thief. He's not into shit like that!"

"I don't think you know your son very well. Let me explain something to you. I sent my nephew here to purchase something for me. Instead, he was beaten and robbed. The money was sent by Bitcoin. After paying a hefty price for a hacker to trace it… it led me to your son's crypto wallet."

Aries frowned, looking at the man like he was crazy. She was confused, mad, and scared all at the same time. Her onslaught of emotions had her puzzled. Before she could even respond, Diaz nodded his head, while looking at his goon that stood behind her. Instantly, the goon looked back towards the staircase and whistled. That's when Aries heard footsteps. She instantly looked back at the stairs and saw Trey coming down. She gasped when she saw the man behind him with a gun to the back of his head with his finger on the trigger.

"Show her," Diaz said, casually sliding his hands into his pocket.

The goon pulled out the phone and showed a screenshot of the sender and receiver of the large amount of money. Aries instantly noticed her son's cash app handle. She had sent him money numerous times, so she knew it by heart. The gunman and Trey had made their way to Aries. The sight of the gun to her son's head made her instantly lower her gun. The goon shoved Trey and he ended up in the arms of his mom. She immediately hugged him and then examined his face, making sure they didn't put a hand on him.

She still had the gun in her hands as she wrapped her arms around him, so the goon snatched it out of her hands.

Aries quickly shot her eyes to her empty hand and knew that she had fucked up. She would never slip like that, but her son being in danger rattled her. It was the double M tattooed on her hand and that symbolized who she really was. Aries was disappointed in herself because she knew better. She also understood that Diaz didn't know who she was either because if he did, he wouldn't be in her house.

She wrapped one hand around her son and focused her attention on Diaz, knowing that he had the upper hand. She had a piercing stare as she looked at the charming, older gentleman.

"Go head. Ask him," Diaz said as he nodded his head in the direction of Trey.

"Trey, what's dis bout, eh?" Aries said as she looked into his eyes.

Trey's head dropped when his mother gazed at him. Aries knew her son like the back of her hand and by his mannerisms, she knew that he was guilty of what he was accused of. She understood that he had done exactly what Diaz claimed.

"How could yu' be so stupid, eh?" she said under her breath as she placed her hands on his cheek. She was heartbroken. She had spent years sheltering him and doing her best to keep him out of harm's way, but she came to understand that it wasn't enough.

"It wasn't me. Crow said that he would..." Trey said nervously as he tried to explain himself.

"Crow?" Aries asked in confusion. She knew that Crow was nothing but trouble and was confused.

"Where is the money? Transfer it back right now."

She then focused her attention on Diaz and got to business. She took a deep breath and closed her eyes as she exhaled. She instantly thought about rectifying the situation. If her son wasn't involved, she would have been plotting murder. However, the circumstances...

"How much? We can take care of this. Then yu' can get de' fuck out of me house."

"I don't want your money," Diaz replied. Aries' eyes squinted in confusion as she tried to understand Diaz's angle.

"Well, what chu want?" she asked.

"I want your restaurant."

"What?"

"I want you to wash my money. This island is the most traveled through. People from the U.S.

love coming here, so that means heavy traffic. Cash transactions. And you, my friend, have the most popular establishment on the island," Diaz explained.

"I don't know de' first thing about washing money. Why me? I can just pay you de' money," Aries spat.

"I know you don't. That's why I will teach you. I will show you how to launder money. After a little research, I've learned that I have hit the jackpot the moment I placed my foot on this great soil you have."

"Yu' have de' wrong person. Me just trying to make a living, live quietly, and stay out of de' way."

"I beg to differ. I have the right person, correct? Murder Mama?" Diaz said as he glanced down at Aries' hand and focused on the tattoo that pledged her allegiance for life to her sisters.

"You are the only member that got off unscathed. That means you were the smart one." Aries wanted to deny who she really was, but it seemed like he had done his homework on her. She remained silent.

"You are her. You're also on the FBI's most wanted list back in the States. I'm pretty sure they would love the news that you are in the islands hiding out."

Aries had had enough of people wanting to wash money through her business. What she was finding out was the island had always been the number one destination for criminals to wash and hide dirty money.

"Are yu' threatening me?" Aries probed, but this time she had a scowl on her face. She felt disrespected.

"See, I like that. You have that fire that's needed to be a great partner," Diaz said, smiling. He loved the fiery spirit of Aries and it made him realize that he had made the right decision to choose her.

"Partner," Aries said. She then looked at Trey and whispered to him to go upstairs. She was now clicked on and she felt the old her coming out. Trey didn't know what was going on and had a look of confusion.

"Now," Aries said aggressively through her tightly clenched teeth. He had never heard his mother use that tone. He did what she said and headed back upstairs, brushing past Diaz's goons. The goons looked at Diaz to see what he wanted to do. Diaz held up his hand and sent a demand under his breath.

"It's ok," he whispered as he shot them a look, indicating that it was ok and to let him by without any push back. Aries watched her son go up the stairs and out of her sight before she focused back on Diaz.

"I'm listening," Aries stated.

"I produce and distribute a new synthetic drug called fentanyl. It gives you the ability to make any drug stronger if mixed correctly. It's also one hundred times more potent than morphine and it was created as an opioid to help cancer patients. However, we all know a good thing never stays a good thing, now does it?" he stated.

"De' fuck is this? Me not the bitch to sell drugs. Or wash drug money," Aries appealed, trying to get Diaz to see that he was making a mistake by propositioning her.

"No... you are the bitch to wash my money. It's hands off for you. I'll set up shop on the island and the only thing you have to do is cook the books for me," Diaz said, speaking in laundering lingo. "My accountant will handle everything. He knows what we are doing and how to launder. Plus, you'll get a hefty token of my appreciation. Twenty percent of what gets washed goes into your pocket. And I believe that's a great deal, being that your son stole from me."

"Fuck yu'," Aries said, knowing that she was put in a position that placed her between a rock and a hard place.

"And it's that other thing..." Diaz said as he walked towards Aries and stopped right beside her. Aries' cover was blown and her past had finally caught up with her. She had no choice but to agree to Diaz's offer. He whispered, "My accountant will be here Friday to set everything up. Have a good night."

Aries froze and didn't say anything as she heard her clip being ejected from her gun. The goon tossed her gun on the couch and kept the clip as the crew followed Diaz out of the door. They left Aries standing there stuck in disbelief as her world was suddenly turned upside down.

"Fuckkk!" she yelled as she plopped down on the couch while shaking her head. She knew that she had just made a deal with the devil.

Chapter Nine

MURDA MAMA FOR LIFE

There was an early morning fog and moistness in the air. Sheriff Gipson approached the precinct with his keys in hand. He unlocked the door, and his attention immediately focused on the small holding cell where Flower slept. He saw her doodling in a coloring book one of the locals had given her.

"Morning, Flower!" Gip said as he threw his keys on the desk. Flower looked over at Gip and smiled. Gip walked to the cell and smiled at Flower. She had grown on him, and he genuinely looked at her like a granddaughter. He hated that she slept in the precinct, but she couldn't get comfortable anywhere else. He had tried his house, but she seemed uneasy. He even convinced the local hotel to give her a room for a flat monthly fee, which he offered to pay. Still, Flower didn't like that either. She felt at home there, so Gip decided to let Flower have it her way.

"I just ordered us some breakfast; it should be here in about twenty minutes," he said as he took his seat at his desk and began to get settled. "Your favorite… oatmeal with brown sugar and fruit."

Flower put the crayon down and clapped gleefully. He looked over at the bed and then smiled. Flower was undeveloped in most of her thinking; however, she always made her bed up military style every time. The sheets were so tight and flat that a quarter could bounce off it. He assumed whatever family member who raised her taught her that, and it stuck. In fact, she always kept the cell clean and intact despite her wild appearance. That part about Flower always impressed Gip. He walked over and put his hand on her shoulder.

"Okay, sweetheart, I'm about to start the day. If you need me, you know where to find me."

Flower nodded and then focused back on her book to begin coloring. Gip walked out and headed to his desk. He looked around and noticed something odd. The file cabinet was slightly opened. He instantly squinted his eyes and walked towards it. The opening was very slight; however, he knew how he had left things. It… wasn't… how… he left it.

It was the profile drawer. That drawer was the most important on the island because it was where he kept the island's non-natives. Usually, it was the town's money launderers. It wasn't the smartest thing, just something he had been doing over the years. At his age, it was hard keeping up with all his monetary cuts. He walked up to the file cabinet and paused as he thought long and hard.

"Flower. Sweetheart," he said as he headed back to the cell where she was. He stood at the entrance and looked at Flower. He continued. "Did you mess with my file cabinet?"

She quickly shook her head sideways frantically, signaling no.

"Hmm, that's odd," Gip said as he folded his arms and gently pinched his chin like a thinking man.

"Wait, did somebody come in here last night?" Gip asked, knowing that was the only logical explanation. He knew Flower wouldn't lie to him. She shook her head up and down quickly, confirming what he already knew.

"Who was it?" Gip asked as he walked to Flower and put his hand on her shoulder. She just looked up at him with lost eyes. He knew that she wouldn't be able to answer him. He took a deep breath and smiled at her.

"I know you can't communicate that to me. Don't worry; Ol' Gip will get to the bottom of it," he said just before he left out the cell and headed to the front door. He walked to the rear of the station and saw that the lock had been broken on the backdoor.

"That's how they got in right there," he said as he ran his hand along the bent metal. It looked like it had been pried open by a crowbar.

"God damn it!" he said through his clenched teeth. He returned to the evidence room to check what had been stolen. He flicked on the light and walked to where the few guns were stored. To his surprise, nothing was missing. The town didn't have much crime outside white-collared ones, so there wasn't much there.

"Hmm," he said to himself as he again folded his arms and went into a thinking mode. He slowly turned around, scanning the room, hopefully finding some clue. He just couldn't wrap his mind around who would come in but not take anything. He instantly thought about Flower. His stomach dropped in worry of someone bothering Flower when they broke in.

"Did someone touch you?" Gip asked with deep concern. Flower shook her head no rapidly. Gip walked to her and gingerly bent his knees to be eye-to-eye with her.

"Now, tell me the truth. Did someone come in here and bother you," he repeated.

Still, Flower shook her head. Just as Gip was about to ask another question, the bell chimed, then walked in two unfamiliar faces. Gip stood up and walked around his desk to greet them. His hands rested on his waistline where his gun was for easy access.

A tall, slim black man was the first to greet Gip. The man had a shiny bald head and was fair skinned. He had a salt and pepper goatee and looked to be in his mid-fifties. Gip immediately saw the badge on his beltline; a federal badge.

"Good morning. How may I help you?" Sherriff Gipson greeted them as they approached.

"Nice to meet you, sir. I'm Detective Watson, and this is Detective Valdez. We are with the Federal Bureau of Investigations." He opened his hand and motioned to his partner; the short Latino woman. She looked to be in her forties and had a stern look; she was very serious. Her expression said, "I don't fuck around." She wasn't a beauty queen, but she wasn't bad on the eyes either. She had a couple of extra pounds around her waist, but the attractiveness was still there.

"This is my partner, Gena Vasquez."

"Okay, how may I help you?" Gip said as he reached over and shook their hands one by one.

"Well, you have a fugitive on the island, but we're having trouble locating her," Watson said.

"Not sure what you're talking about. Help me understand what that has to do with me if there is a "fugitive"... you say that's here on the island," Gip replied.

"Well, sir, it has a lot to do with you. Let's sit down and have a talk?" Suggested Detective Watson.

"Sure, have a seat," Gip said as he quickly waved them towards the two chairs.

Vasquez followed. Gip walked back around his desk and took a seat. He leaned forward and collapsed his hands on the desk.

"How may I help you?" Gip questioned with a friendly smile.

"No, the question is... how can we help you?" Watson said as he placed his briefcase on the floor and reached down to open it up. He pulled out a few pieces of paper and put them in front of Gip. Gip looked down at the pictures, and his heart instantly dropped. There were surveillance photos of him walking in and out of a casino with regular clothes on and a baseball cap pulled low.

"What the hell is this? What are these pictures

supposed to mean?" Gip asked with irritation in his voice and demeanor.

"Well, the pictures don't mean too much. It's what you do when you get there," Detective Vasquez interjected.

"That's still not telling me anything," Gip said, defending himself.

"Sherriff, cut the bullshit. We know that you're helping people launder money. You're taking your cut and trying to clean your money by going to the casino, swapping them out for chips, only to give them back. Then when you cash out, you ask for a check in return."

"What the fuck is that supposed to be? That doesn't prove anything," Gip said aggressively as he pushed the photos back to their side of the table.

"Okay, I want you to look at something else," Detective Watson said. He reached down into his bag again. This time he pulled out bank statements. By the logo at the top of the paper, Gip knew they were his.

"Here are your deposits from the checks at the casino. This past year you've totaled more than one point two million dollars. I'd say that's a hefty totally for someone who makes only forty grand a year on a cop's salary."

"Like I said, I gamble," Gip responded. Now he

was perturbed.

"Okay, even if that's so. We have enough to put you in the can for tax evasion. It says here you haven't paid in ten years," Watson said. Gip instantly dropped his head and knew he had made a mistake along his hustle. He knew that bad times were ahead for him. He was caught red-handed.

"But we don't want you," Vasquez interjected as she put her hand on the pictures. Gip looked up at the lady and turned his head in frustration.

"What?"

"You heard me. We don't want you or the other sixteen business owners that wash money in this town. We want the Queen. We want the Cartel Queen... Aries."

"Aries?" Gip said as if he had never heard the name.

"Look, stop fucking around. You know exactly who she is. We know she's here somewhere, but we can't locate her for some reason. She does a great job of staying under the radar. We've been looking at her for years, and it never dawned on us that maybe she would've come home... here."

"I don't know shit about no God damn Aries," Gip shot back. He knew by turning Aries in, he might as well pick out a casket for him, his wife, or anybody close to him. Aries wasn't to be played with. However, he still played dumb.

"You know exactly who she is, motherfucker. We must admit, you guys have been hiding her good. We have no videos, recent pictures, or even a trace of her being alive," Watson said as he stared intensely at Gip.

"Well, why in the fuck are you here?" Gip asked, needing help understanding their angle.

"Because we know she's here. We've had an agent on her for quite a while. Our mole has confirmed that she is alive and well. The cover is blown."

Gip's head dropped, knowing that he wasn't bluffing. He already knew where the leak came from. The local bar, Jimmy's, couldn't keep steady waitresses because he was so damn cheap. Jimmy had different faces running his bar for what seemed like every month. Also, he hired people that were outside of the island and weren't natives. The island's people protected one another, but Jimmy and his cheapness opened them up to be infiltrated.

"Before you try to hide this woman, let me enlighten you. She's a fucking serial killer. She's killed more people than we can count. She was a paid-for-hire hitter. What's lower than that, huh? She was the number one hitman for the Cartel of

Miami."

"Look…" Gip began to speak as he threw up his hands, signaling he had no information to give.

"Look, nothing. She's here, and we know it!"

Gip didn't let the information sway his opinion of Aries because he knew her heart. She only killed terrible people and drug dealers at war with one another. The twisted picture that Watson was painting was not that of Aries. But Gip had to suppress his emotions and act like he was getting new information. He listened closely as Watson continued.

"Her whole crew is either dead or in jail. She is the final piece. They called themselves the Murda Mamas," Watson said as a sense of euphoria came over him. He had a hard-on for Aries and her capture. It was like a trophy for Watson. In his eyes, he had one more to put on his mantel before he retired.

"I don't know what you're talking about. So, if you guys don't have anything else to say besides this… I have a town to look over. Good day people," Gip said as he stood up and extended his hand.

Watson and his partner stood up and returned the gesture. After they shook, Watson reached into his inner coat pocket and pulled out a business card. He laid it on Gip's desk, and then they headed out, leaving Gip perplexed and worried. He had to find the island's mole and then talk with Aries. Shit was heading south, and it was running there fast.

Chapter Ten

THREE WAY

Every single square of floor space in Aries' living room was covered with white and red roses. It seemed like a hundred dozen roses filled the room. Aries stood at the bottom of the step, stunned and overwhelmed with joy. It looked like she was in a gigantic field of roses. A strong, fresh scent circulated through the room, and Aries had never smelled a rose scent so strong. A single card was sticking out of the vase closet to the stairs. Aries bent over and picked the card out of the vase. She unfolded it, and it read:

I would love to lie to you sometimes...

-Saint

Aries smiled at his cleverness. She picked up a rose and inhaled it deeply with her eyes closed. She loved how the fresh scent took over her senses, making her feel brief euphoria. Just as she focused on the beautiful sea of red and white colors, she heard a knock on the door. She was on high alert because of the surprise visit from Diaz, so her eyes quickly shot to the door. She quickly pulled the gun from her robe's pocket and switched off the safety. She walked over to the front window and slightly pulled the curtains back. She peeked at the front porch and then sighed in relief. It was Sherriff Gipson and Flower.

Flower stood behind him, twiddling her fingers while Gip stood there in full uniform and his hands on his belt. Aries instantly let her guard down and tucked her gun under the couch's pillow. She went to open the door and greeted Gip.

"Morning Gip. What do me owe this pleasant surprise, eh?" Aries said as she leaned into her doorway and looked into his eyes. "Hey, Flower," she added as she looked past Gip to speak to her girl. Flower didn't react much; she just glanced and smiled a bit. She rushed over to the roses on the floor and sat right in the middle, playing with the petals, and trying to smell each rose. She handled each one with pure joy on her face.

"I tried to come to talk to you alone, but she kept following me, wanting to tag along," Gip said, looking down at Flower, who was in her own world.

Gip focused back on Aries and continued. "We

have trouble in paradise," he said in his long drawl.

"What's that supposed to mean?" Aries asked, trying to understand precisely what Gip was saying.

"I got two federal agents in my office, trying to find out where you are."

"Wait… what?" Aries said, trying to wrap her mind around what was just told to her.

"That's right. The city slickers came in with their fancy suits and uppity talk asking for the last Murder Mama."

"What did you tell them?" Aries asked, immediately jumping on the defense, not knowing who to trust.

"I didn't tell them squat. That's for shit-sure. We live by a code in this town and will continue that. Now, if it was one of these out-of-towners, I would've given em' up quicker than sand. But they weren't looking for them… they were looking for you," Gip said as he pointed his finger and gently pressed the middle of Aries' chest.

"Fuck!" Aries said as she dropped her head. Her mind began to race. She knew that this time would eventually come. It wasn't a coincidence that they went around the same time that her friend slash former partner in crime was being released from prison.

Miamor was already in custody for their past crimes; however, they were letting her out early because of a bill passed by Donald Trump; the bill that let prisoners get out because of Covid-19. Miamor's political connections were worked from the inside, and magically her name popped up on the list of recipients eligible for release. One-half of the Murda Mamas was coming home. This was great news; however, it shined the light on Aries; the only member at large from the infamous Miami crew she was a part of.

"You don't have to worry. I didn't tell them anything. They said they know you are on the island but they are building a case. See, that's how they do. Especially if you have enough money to fight them. They would rather watch you until you slip and do something concrete so they can prosecute you with confidence. That's what they're trying to do with you I believe," Gip said as he placed both hands on her shoulders. He looked directly into her eyes and continued.

"Look, we are going to protect and harbor you. You're not one of these fly by nights, leeching folks that come here, squeeze our economy, and head back to whatever hell hole they came from. You are one of us. You are ours, and we intend on acting like it," Gip assured her.

"Me don't understand why they just didn't come get me if they know I'm here. They can't fuck with me, right?" Aries asked.

"That's the thing... they can. We fall under the 2002 Extradite Treaty. Before then, people came here all the time to gain freedom, but things changed."

"Fuck!" Aries said under her breath and looked away.

Gip felt bad seeing Aries in distress. He could see on her face that her mind was working. Aries was tough as nails, but he knew this news shook her. Not for herself but for her son. An extra wave of guilt overcame Gip, knowing he had left out that they had a mole on the island. He had an idea where the mole was placed but decided to withhold that info from Aries. If something happened, he didn't want to be the person that provided the bad news to her. He knew Aries believed in killing the messenger and was aware of her capabilities. Aries was what you called a connoisseur of murder. He wanted no part of her wrath.

On the other hand, Aries put a plan together to protect herself and her family. She had her hands full with the newfound feds on her and the Diaz situation.

***

Saint sat at the bar and sipped on a glass of cognac. He looked around, scoping the scenery, which justified his plan. The bar was packed. Unlike the night that he was there before, the place was jumping. The music was louder, the lights were dimmer, and they had a DJ controlling the crowd. It was like a Caribbean-styled rave party. People were drunk, dancing, and having a good time to the island vibes. He was waiting for the owner to come out and sit with him. He requested to see him to talk about potential business. Once Aries introduced him to the bar, his mind began to churn. Just as he took another sip, Jimmy came out from the back office. Jimmy was in his late fifties, overweight, and white. His hair was pulled back into a ponytail, and he had a receding hairline, exposing his near-bald front.

At first glance, Jimmy looked like he was of Italian descent, and his tan gave his skin an orange hue. He wore a Hawaiian shirt with the first few buttons undone, exposing his protruding chest hairs. Jimmy looked at Saint, smiling as he approached from behind the bar.

"Hey, is everything okay? I heard you asked for the owner," Jimmy said smugly.

"Yeah, I wondered if we could talk," Saint said as he reached down at the cloth napkin in front of him. He slid it towards Jimmy, then slightly peeled the napkin back, just enough for Jimmy to see the cash-filled envelope underneath.

"Of course, we can. Step into my office," Jimmy said as he threw his head towards the back.

Jimmy headed to the back, and Saint followed right after. Just as he reached the door, Red came from the kitchen with food on a tray. They caught the eyes of each other, and she ran her tongue across her top lip. Saint paused and looked as she passed him. His eyes followed her ass as she went onto the floor to serve her customers. Saint had thoughts run through his mind, and flashbacks of her pleasuring Aries at the back of the bar emerged. As a gentleman, he couldn't let her walk back alone after being out with him. His conscious wouldn't let him. He thought he would see Aries home safe, but he got a peep show instead. He watched Aries' facial expressions and immediately knew she liked it there. That was her space where she felt complete bliss. He made a mental note of that.

Saint focused on the business at hand and stepped into Jimmy's office. Jimmy sat behind his desk and leaned back in his chair, waiting for Saint.

"You got my attention," he said, cutting straight to the point. "Have a seat," he offered.

"Nah, I'm good. I'll stand," Saint said smoothly as he stood in front of him and crossed his hands in front of his body.

"Fair enough," Jimmy replied.

"My name is Saint Von. I own the teen spot by the docks," Saint said.

"Nice to meet you, Saint Von," Jimmy said satirically.

"Just Saint is cool," Saint said non-aggressively. Jimmy nodded his head, taking note. Saint continued. "I love your establishment, and I can see us doing some good business."

"Okay, will this business get me more envelopes like this?" Jimmy said as he picked up the envelope and thumbed through the bills.

"Absolutely. It's more where that came from."

"What you wanna do? Wash? I got two guys running lettuce through here, so you must get in line. If that's what you're looking for," Jimmy said, shaking his head, holding his hands out, and gesturing that was nothing he could do. Jimmy had been using his business for fronts for years. Actually, it was the reason he moved to the island. The mafia used to run through the Caribbeans for years, and although the mafia was over, the blueprints were still the same.

"Nah, I wanna put a couple of my guys in here,

JaQuavis Coleman

and you know... do a little work. Pills," Saint said bluntly.

"So, you wanna peddle pills through the bar?"

"Yeah, but I wanna do it hiding in plain sight. I want people to come to the bar and order a new drink with a little something on the side. Feel me? Long story short... you'll have a few secret items on ya' menu."

"Wait, lemme get this right. Do you want this to be a store? For illegal pills?"

"Bingo. That's exactly what I want."

"You sound like a fool," Jimmy said as he shook his head, knowing it would make his bar too hot.

"My young boys been doing it at the teen club, and it's a flawless operation. I just don't give kids drugs, so it's time to graduate," Saint explained.

"The Wave?"

"That's right," Saint answered. At that moment, Jimmy began to reconsider. He kept his ear to the street, and not once had he heard about drugs being run through The Wave. That's what intrigued him because nothing usually got past him.

"If I did do this... what's my cut?" Jimmy inquired.

"Twenty percent. I put one of my soldiers behind the bar, and your staff doesn't have to know anything about it."

"Twenty-five percent," Jimmy said in rebuttable.

"Twenty percent," Saint said firmly. Jimmy paused for a second, not loving Saint's sturdiness. However, he respected it.

"Okay... twenty. But I want a twenty-five-thousand-dollar advance.

"That's what I gave you in that envelope."

"I need another one."

Saint paused and did the math. He knew he would make that in a week if Jimmy let him stretch his legs out and hustle.

"Bet." Saint responded. They shook hands, and the deal was done. Saint headed out of the office with a new perspective. He began thinking about how he would set up shop and do what he did best; get money.

Saint made his way through the hot and muggy crowd. Crow was close by, following him as usual. Saint always moved militant, and that night was no different. He saw Red headed towards the rear of the bar and slipped out the back. Saint wanted to bump into her so he could properly introduce himself. He needed all the allies he could get if he was going to start getting money at the establishment.

Saint went to the back and slid out. He saw Red sitting on the same stoop she was on the night she had a freaky encounter with Aries. She was smoking a cigarette with her head down, looking at her cell phone.

"Red, right?" Saint said, startling her. She looked up quickly and then smiled shortly after. She put away her phone and took a drag of the cigarette she held between her middle and index finger. She tooted her big, red lips to the side and blew out smoke.

"Yeah, that's me," she answered.

"Need some company?" Saint asked as he grinned. He flashed his pretty white teeth over the row of gold slugs. Red loved Saint's look. She loved his boss' belly and the bulge in his pants. She scooted over, giving him room to sit next to her. Saint took the hint and walked around, then he sat down.

"How you doing tonight?" Saint asked as he watched Red put out her cigarette on the step.

"I'm doing good, handsome. You?" she asked.

"I can't complain. I'm Saint Von. But people just call me Saint," he said.

"Aw shit..." Red said as she smiled and shook her head.

"What?" Saint responded, grinning as well.

"My mama told me to never trust a nigga with two first names."

Saint nodded his head and agreed.

"I have heard that before. But I'm solid, baby. You gots to know that," he responded.

"You smooth, huh?"

"That's what they say," he said.

"Alright, Saint. See you one of those slick niggas," she said.

"Nah, I'm a straight shooter. You new around here, right?"

"Yeah. Just sticking around to save some money. I won't be here long."

"You in and out, huh?" Saint said.

"Yep. I'mma finish my book, go to New York, and get me a deal."

"Oh, so you're a writer?" he asked.

"For sure."

Saint nodded his head as if he was impressed. "Dope... dope."

"I got a little crush on your friend," Red said, being blunt and direct.

"I can tell."

"I don't know too many people here, so I'm looking for a friend... or two," Red said as she turned and looked at Saint. The way she said that to Saint, she was making it known that she was with the shits. She was very sexual and didn't try to hide it. Red was a certified freak, and the fact that she wasn't getting steady sex really had her on edge. She had an itch that really needed to be scratched.

"So, you like women?"

"I like to cum," she said, cutting to the chase.

"Oh shit," Saint said as he rubbed his hand over his head , not knowing how to respond to her. The average man would have tried to bend Red over right at that moment, but Saint had other plans. Saint wanted Aries on the business tip, but he also was attracted to her mind and body. He wanted her for multiple reasons. He knew immediately that Red might be an excellent tool to get closer to her.

"Maybe we all can be friends," Red said as she stood up. Her ass jiggled in her stretch pants, and Saint's eyes shot directly at it. He imagined having her and Aries at the same time. But he knew that was far-fetched. He shook his head and only imagined.

"I like how that sounds," Saint replied. Red walked to the back door, and Saint stood up and called to her. "Aye!" he yelled as she approached the door.

"I'mma be around a little more. Me and Jimmy got some business, so I'll see you around."

Red smiled and then disappeared back into the bar. Saint smiled and knew that he was on to something. Red was attractive, and he planned on digging more. Saint paused for a second and begin to think about the possibility. His mind instantly went to a threesome with the two women, but he quickly shook that notion off and told himself he should focus on the business side of the situation. He wanted Aries to clean his money, but he wouldn't mind if she cleaned something else off him as well.

Saint felt the urge to piss and so he saw the dumpster not too far from him. He decided to relieve himself behind it. He walked briskly over to it while unbuckling his pants. He then began pulling his pole out and letting that water go. He pissed hard like a racehorse and threw his head back, relieved, as he drained his bladder.

Saint was so busy pissing; he didn't notice the two guys approaching him. Both wore all-black and had on ski masks. One of the men was about 6'6" and well over three hundred pounds, while the other guy was a tad shorter but stocky. By the time Saint put his junk back in his pants, it was too late. One of the masked men bear-hugged him, pinning his arms to his side so Saint couldn't grab his gun from his waist, while the other man threw a black pillowcase over his head. Saint could tell that they were white by the skin that showed in the holes in the eye openings of the ski mask. The big burly man grabbed Saint and whispered in his ear.

"If you make one move or a noise, my partner is going to blow your fuckin' head off your shoulders," the burly man said. After his statement, Saint felt something solid being pressed against his head followed by the sound of the hammer being cocked back. Saint slowly nodded his head up and down.

"Okay," he said in a low tone. He then felt a hand reach into his waistline and relieved him of his Glock that he had tucked. Saint had no idea what was going on and he was waiting for a shot to go off and he was sure it was his time to go. He couldn't believe that he would die because of sloppiness and not being on point. He was at the mercy of these two strangers that he knew nothing about. His mind raced, trying to think who he had wronged or had an issue with but nobody came to mind.

"Listen, you have the wrong mu'fucka," Saint said in the most non-intimidating tone. However, he was burning mad on the inside.

"Yea, what the fuck ever," one of the men said. Saint couldn't see shit from under the pillowcase. He felt the man grab him by the back of his neck and guided him around the corner, where a black luxury sprinter van was waiting. The side door was already open.

Saint was tossed into the truck roughly as the masked man finally released him from the bear hug. He instantly heard the faint sounds of Frank Sinatra and smelled the scent of new leather. One of the goons slid in next to him and placed the gun to his ribs and heard the sound of sliding doors coming from both sides. Saint felt the other man on the opposite side. The van took off quickly and Saint felt the bag getting snatched off his head. Saint was confused and didn't understand what was going on.

"Good evening, Saint," an older gentleman in a white linen suit said. He had a heavy tan and slicked back hair.

"What the fuck going on?" Saint asked calmly as he looked to his left and right, and then back at the man in front of him. Their seats were facing each other, so the older man was directly in front of Saint.

"My name is Diaz and I wanted to have a conversation with you," Diaz said, giving him a smile as if he didn't kidnap him. To him, it was just another day in the office.

"You wanted to have a conversation?" Saint asked, not believing what he was hearing. He was confused about this entire encounter. He never seen this man a day in his life. Saint became angrier by the second.

"This isn't how men talk. You could've approached me like a man and talked about whatever you wanted to, respectfully. This way isn't going to end up good for you," Saint threatened, not caring if he would die. At that point, he was willing to get killed over his demand for respect; over his manhood.

"Me?" Diaz asked while pointing his finger into his own chest.

"Yeah... you."

"Well, no disrespect. But this way was so much more fun," Diaz said, making his henchmen chuckle at his joke. However, Saint didn't find it funny at all. Murder was on his mind and he still was trying to figure out what did this old man want from him.

"Why am I here?" Saint asked, getting tired of the games that were being played.

"I've been really enjoying myself on this island lately. The town is like the Vegas of the Caribbeans. So many opportunities. So many laundry mats. Places like this make an old man like me happy. It's a criminal's dream to come here and prepare his exit from any game that he's in," Diaz explained.

"You want me to wash some money for you? That ain't my game. I apply pressure, not get pressure applied. You must find somebody else to squeeze. It ain't going to be me or my establishment."

"I'm not trying to squeeze you. I want to partner with you. I want to expand your business," Diaz explained.

"I'm not looking for partners. You can't do nothing for me."

"I know what you're moving. I know how much you're moving. I know where you're moving it. I'm just trying to show you a bigger world. You see. My entire family is in the business of drugs. Anything you're getting, most likely is coming from someone in my network. So that means I could get it for pennies on your dollar. I've done my research on you and this town. I'm going to be around for a while so it would behoove you to play nice."

"You're asking me or telling me?' Saint said as he didn't have one ounce of fear inside of his heart. Diaz showed humbleness and leaned forward and clasped his hand into one another.

"Listen, I'm not trying to rain on your parade or stop anything that you are doing. I just like what you're doing and I saw an avenue to take where we could help each other out."

"How you figure I even need any help?" Saint asked cool, calm, and collected.

"Because I know that you're paying two dollars a pill, no matter what quantity you buy or what you buy. That's your wholesale price, correct?" Diaz asked as he sat back in his seat and crossed his legs.

How in the fuck did he know that? Saint asked himself as he grimaced in disbelief. Saint immediately began to wonder who this old man was sitting across from him who knew he and his plug's business.

"Yeah, that sounds about right," Saint confirmed.

"See, I know you're wondering how I knew that," Diaz suggested. "Like I said, at the highest level of drug trafficking, it's a very small world."

"So how much can you get them for?" Saint asked, interested to know the number Diaz would say.

"See, that's the thing. We can make them. It cost us around five cents each pill. Now, you can become the plug and stop playing in the kiddie pool. This will open your network up and we can produce the pills here and start taking over the Miami import/export."

"Make the pills?" Saint asked, now that had his

ears perked.

"Exactly. I have a similar operation in Miami but it gets shut down every other month. Being on U.S. soil has its downside and that's the main one. We have to set up shop in different locations every month. That's not good for business," Diaz explained.

"That sounds good, but my guys are street niggas. They don't know anything about making pills," Saint replied.

"That's where my team comes in. I have a group of scientists and pharmacists readily available. They know all the right amounts and concoctions to make anything we need synthetic. Including fentanyl."

When the word fentanyl came out of Diaz's mouth, Saint's mind began to work and churn. He knew that it was the most sought after drug. Fentanyl did a number of things. Most people cut their dope with it to make it stretch, but when used in pills correctly, it increased its potency, which made batches more popular and sought after. This was the recipe for getting a lot of money. Saint understood that fully. Under normal circumstances, this would be a dopeboy's dream; however, Diaz's approach didn't sit too well with Saint. However, Saint wasn't a dummy. He didn't want to cut off his nose to spit in his face. So, instead of immediately turning down the offer, he remained quiet to see how things would unfold. Diaz could see the consideration in Saint's eyes and smiled.

"This town is good people like me. So, I took it upon myself to buy into the resort at the bay. The Lolita... you know where that is, right?"

"Yeah, I know," Saint said. The Lolita was one of the less popular resorts that only naive tourists stayed at and was a sore eye spot for the island.

"I plan to give it a new feel. A little renovation and TLC and it'll be a destination spot. So, needless to say... I'll be around."

"Thanks for the news," Saint said coldly with sarcasm in his tone.

"With that, I'll let you sleep on it. Maybe we could have breakfast to discuss," Diaz said as he gave the driver a hand signal. Within a minute's time, they were at Saint's house, dropping him off in front. Diaz was playing unspoken mind games by dropping Saint off. Diaz wanted him to know that he knew exactly where he lived.

"Maybe your grandma can whip us up something," Diaz added.

Diaz's comment served as more of a threat than a friendly suggestion concerning Saint's grandmother. Saint wanted to check Diaz, but he had to play the game and hold his cards. He was outnumbered and at the place where he laid his head. Saint stepped out of the van, and then he turned to look at Diaz. Saint remained silent as he stared at the man, smiling at him as if he didn't catch the snide comment. An awkward silence filled the air between them and Saint decided to walk off. He wanted to go check on Lovey and then he had some important decisions to make.

Just as he reached the door, Diaz's van pulled out. Moments later, Crow and his crew pulled up and immediately jumped out. Crow looked down the street at the can that had just turned off the block. He didn't know what was going on and he was lost. He walked up to the porch as he threw his hands up in confusion.

Saint shook his head in disappointment and just walked in the house. He closed the door in Crow's face, leaving him there looking stupid in front of his crew. Crow stood there in disbelief, taking a mental note of the disrespect.

Chapter Eleven

DEAD ROSES AND CLOSED CASKETS

ip sat at his desk and read the newspaper while sipping on his morning coffee; his daily routine. He looked over at the empty cell and wondered where was Flower. She had been missing for about a week and he told himself that if she didn't show up by that evening, he would search the town looking for her. Sometimes she would disappear and because she was non-verbal, she couldn't tell him where she had stayed. So he didn't even know where to start. But now, he was beginning to get worried. It had been almost two weeks since the feds came into his office and he battled with himself, knowing that they wanted to jam up Aries. He had known Aries since she was a little girl and the thought of deceiving her was weighing heavy on his heart.

Gip heard a chime and his attention went to the front entrance. He saw the three people walk in. Both FBI agents that had initially approached him were leading the way.

"Good morning, Sheriff," Watson said as he led the way.

Just as the Sherriff was about to respond, he saw the third person coming up the rear. It was a woman with her hair neatly pulled back with diamond stud earrings. She had on light make-up with a friendly face. Her slacks fit tightly and her blouse was neatly tucked in her pants. A big FBI badge was on her waistline as she approached the front desk. Sherriff Gipson was frozen in disbelief. The woman finally spoke with a southern accent.

"Hello, Sherriff Gipson," she said. Sherriff Gipson just stared at her without saying a word and his face dropped to the floor at the woman's appearance. He couldn't believe his eyes. It was Flower. IT... WAS... FLOWER.

She wasn't mentally undeveloped, she wasn't mute, and she wasn't childlike. She was a grown, professional, FBI agent. She was highly intelligent, skilled, and had been putting on a role for months. The island of Barbados had been so corrupt over the years. It harbored so many American criminals that an internal investigation had been launched and Flower was the head of the operation. Her doctorate in psychology made her the number one candidate to go undercover to expose criminals.

She understood the thinking of people and she played on the human instinct to be protectors of children and fools. She created a persona that embodied both, and that was the character; Flower. She had pulled the wool over everyone's eyes. She was willing to go to the furthest extent to get into the central of the corrupted town and turn it upside down. Flower... no... Detective Wade was a master manipulator. Melissa Wade was her name; daughter of a cop, and a law enforcement prodigy.

"Flower?" Gip asked in confusion as he stood up and put his hands on his waist. His mind couldn't grasp what was in front of him.

"No. My name is Melissa Wade and I'm with the Federal Bureau of Investigations. I was assigned to infiltrate the island's criminal enterprise."

"I... I just can't believe it," Gip said as he tried to make sense of what he was seeing. His eyes saw Melissa but his mind and heart was seeing the young lady that he looked at as if she was his granddaughter. Gip's heart was broken and he felt the most ultimate betrayal.

"Nah... your name is Flower. My babygi..."

Sherriff Gipson stopped mid-sentence and clutched his chest. He let out a grunt and fell back into his chair. His eyes bucked. He strained and moaned in pain. Detective Wade immediately went over to him with worry and concern.

"Sheriff! What's wrong?" she asked as she grabbed him by his shoulders. Her eyes moved frantically, trying to understand what was going on with the sheriff. Detective Wade and Gip locked eyes and his body began to quiver as his body tensed up.

"I think he's having a heart attack," Watson said as he hurried around the desk to get to Gip's aid.

His eyes were bloodshot red and veins began to show in his pupils. Detective Wade was frozen in fear. She felt the overhearing burden of guilt as Gip's life began to slip away. Tears began to form in Detective Wade's eyes and she knew what was to come. Gip's body relaxed and he kept the piercing stare. Detective Wade watched as her former guardian slowly eased back into his chair and his breathing became heavy. Gip held the left side of his chest and clenched his jaws tightly as his life left his body.

"Call the fucking ambulance!" Detective Wade said as she looked back at her partners. She focused back on Gip as a tear slid down her face.

Watson hesitated to call the local dispatch in fear that Detective Wade's cover would be blown, but it was too late. He was gone.

***

Detective Wade and the other two agents sat in the small shop that once was a souvenir shop for the island. It was now a make-shift office for the agents to work from. All the windows were blacked out and the doors were bolted shut. The only way in and out was the secluded rear exit. In the back of the building, there were no other active businesses. It was perfect for someone to run a hub for a sting operation. And that's exactly what they did. Before they got there, their agencies installed a shower and a cozy living area for the agents to be comfortable. It looked like a modest hotel on the inside. They had been there for a few months as they tried to build their cases of the island's corrupt system.

A gigantic board was on the wall with scattered notes, pictures, and a map were pinned on it. Detective Wade had created maps for drug routes and pinpointed the hot spots of the island once she was assigned this case. Her head was blown. The small island was more corrupt than factions in D.C. back in the United States. She had never seen so much organized crime, money laundering, and crime all done so freely. The entire town was like an indictment. The criminals back in the U.S. could come here and do a few things; escape the long arm of the law, wash money, make people disappear, and create a pipeline of illegal drugs.

"So, this who we need to take down. Saint Von. Originally from New Orleans, connections in Cuba, and heavy drug trafficker. I've tried to infiltrate his main hub inside of the town but haven't had any luck. I believe it's the hub that distributes all the drugs at the dock. This dock has over a million tourists a month via cruises and American visitors. I believe this is where he gets his drugs into the U.S."

"Saint Von. What do we have on him back home?" Watson asked and jotted down notes on his pad.

"That's the thing. He's like a walking rumor. He's clean as a whistle and on paper, he just looks like a teen club owner who takes care of his elderly grandmother. Highly intelligent. He has all his tees crossed and I's dotted. A criminal savant," Detective Wade answered.

"Damn. Okay. Got it. Who's this? He looks scary as hell," the other agent asked.

"That's Damon Croswell. Better known as Crow. He is Saint's head general. He's only twenty but has a rap sheet longer than anyone I've ever seen at his age. Robbery, attempted murder, assault with a deadly weapon. You name it, he's done it in some sort of fashion. The local judicial system is so corrupt, nothing ever sticks with this guy."

"He looks like a skinned cat," Watson added and chuckled at his own joke.

"Yeah, but he's a savage. I've never seen anyone like him. He has no conscience and literally has the entire town afraid of him. We can't really touch him because he's not a U.S. citizen. Nonetheless, we have to find a way to utilize him to get to Saint."

"Shifting focus." Detective Wade moved her pen over to the far side of the board with an old mugshot of Aries. Just under her were the original Murder Mamas. All of them with mugshots and a red x over their faces. Everyone except Miamor Jones, who had a mugshot right next to her.

"This woman right here is her partner in crime. They're like sisters. They went from doing petty robberies to eventually graduating to murderers for hire. These two women have street fame and books that were even written about them. Miamor moved her way up and became the Queen of the Miami Cartel, by marrying Carter Jones."

"You're talking about the Carter Jones, Carter

Jones?" Watson asked, confirming she was talking about the notorious drug boss. The man that used to be on the radar of every law informant official in the southern region.

"Yes," Detective Wade simply answered.

"Isn't he dead?" Watson asked.

"Yeah, supposedly. But to be honest, I'm not believing shit until I see that fucker on a coroner's table split open. Then I'd have to see him in the casket being dropped into the dirt," Detective Wade said only half-joking.

The sound of Carter's name brought a coldness to the room and his reputation exceeded himself. He was one of a kind and had the love in the streets that no one had ever seen since BMF.

"Okay, guys let's stay focused, "Detective Wade said as she rested her hand on her holder and gun, turning towards her team.

"We already have Miamor on other charges, but the only one left is our target, Aries," she express-ed.

The sounds of music and noise began to get closer, causing everyone to pause. Detective Wade instantly dropped her head. She didn't want her crew to see the tears that were threatening to fall from her eyes. It was a parade. It was the day of Sheriff Gip's homegoing.

"What's that?" Watson said as she looked back, not being able to see through the covered glass.

It's a celebration. It's the island's tradition to parade the local's body around the island before they reach the gravesite."

Detective Wade felt the guilt and blamed herself for the death of Gip. She gave him the bad news that subsequently led to his fatal heart attack. She turned towards the board and looked at his picture, which was a few inches under Aries.

She grabbed the red marker from the base of the board and put an X on his picture. Just as she did it, a tear finally dropped. She quickly wiped it away and placed the marker down.

"Give me a second," she stated as she left for the backroom, leaving the two agents in the room, looking at one another. They both understood that going undercover for that long had the tendency to change a person. Sometimes when playing a role of someone that you're not, it stuck. It becomes a part of you and sometimes, it carved out a space in your heart. Flower was in Detective Wade's heart.

Chapter Twelve

SAFE HAVENS AND MONEY TREES

Saint, Lovey, Trey, and Aries walked into the house— all wearing their Sunday best. They all had obituaries in their hands. It had been over a week since Gip's death and it shook up the entire island. No one saw it coming and it caught everyone by surprise. They laid his soul to rest on that day.

"He looked like he was sleeping. They did a damn good job sending him home to the Lord," Lovey said as she stopped and looked at Aries, then Trey. "You like sweet potato pie?" Lovey asked as she looked at Trey.

"Yes ma'am," he answered.

"Come on up in here with me. Let me get you a warm slice with some vanilla ice cream. How that sound?" she asked as she lightly pinched his cheek.

Trey nodded his head in agreeance. Lovey then looked to Aries and rubbed her back She added a small grin and warming eyes. With that, she headed to the back.

"Come on, baby," Lovey said and disappeared into the kitchen.

Aries still had tears in her eyes and Saint was surprised. She had been so tough. It felt weird seeing her so vulnerable.

"Hey... you ok?" Saint asked as he gently grabbed her by her shoulders and looked into her yes. Aries nodded her head, signaling yes, but that was a lie. She was broken. She had known Gip since she was a little girl and he was the only piece of her childhood that she had left.

"He was just here. Just here..." Aries shook her head, hating the fact that she didn't have a chance to say goodbye.

"He lived a long life, love. He's in a better place for sure," Saint said as he leaned in to hug her. Aries laid her head on his chest and just melted in his arms. Aries felt the most guilt because she couldn't see him off correctly. She had to play the back and watch from afar, knowing that the feds were on the island according to Gip. The other reason why Gip's death was devastating was because she lost the intel on the feds.

"So much is going on yu' know," Aries admitted as felt his warm embrace. It felt so good to Aries to be in a strong man's arms. She hadn't felt the strength of a man since she had been on the island. She had seen men be the downfall of a woman so much and she was guarded. It honestly was the main thing that strengthened her curiosity of being intimate with a woman. Nevertheless, it felt good with Saint.

"Yu' have no idea of de' shit goin' on, yu' know?"

"Why don't you tell me, love?" Saint suggested as he caressed her back.

"Not right now," Aries responded.

"Everything around me is chaos. Everything," she said, thinking about the feds on her trail. She just wanted to be left alone. All the anxiety of her consequences were in her chest. She just felt overwhelmed. Saint could feel her tense body and wanted to help her. He combed through her mind, trying to figure out a way to help her and a thought emerged.

"Yo, let's just go for a few days," Saint suggested.

"Go where?" Aries asked unauthentically, still burying her face in his chest.

"I have a spot in White Hill that no one knows

about. Maybe we could go there for a day or two. Just so you can get away and clear your head."

"I wish. I can't do dat," Aries responded.

"Why can't you?" Saint questioned as he grabbed her shoulders and leaned back, so he could look into her pretty eyes. Aries gazed into Saint's eyes and felt his genuine concern. This made her feel comfortable with him. It felt so good. It felt like something real.

"I mean... me son's here by himself," Aries said as she looked back to the kitchen area.

"He's a teenager. I'm pretty sure he can take care of himself for a few days," Saint said as he flashed his smile.

"No... yu' don't get it. He's not like other kids. He's not like me. He's timid, yu' know," Aries said being truthful about her humble son.

"Okay, check this out. He can stay with Lovey. She would love somebody around other than me," he said. He gently shook her playfully and then continued. "Just a day or two."

"Okay," she said, knowing that she was due for a getaway, even if it was for a short time.

"Good," Saint said. He was looking forward to connecting with her. He really wanted to help her relax so that's exactly what he planned to do.

***

Aries looked over at Saint and smiled as she rocked in the passenger seat of Saint's trunk. Saint looked over at her and smiled and focused back on the road. Aries was like a little girl as she stared out the window and smiled. Her eyes were shifting, trying to take in the scenic drive. They had driven just outside of the island, where it looked drastically different. Aries looked around and smiled as they made their way down a dirt path. They were in the middle of a rain forest and it was one of the most beautiful things Aries had ever seen. She had no idea that this place existed. The long leaves hung from the tall trees as sunlight slightly peeked through the open slots in between. The vibrant colors of the flowers that grew along the dirt road looked like skittles. The exotic atmosphere gave Aries a feeling of euphoria and stimulated her senses.

She rolled down the window so she could feel the wind. As they rolled, she placed her forearms on the windowsill. She unwrapped her head scarf and stuck her head out the window. Saint looked at her and felt good that she seemed happy. Aries let the wind blow in her face as she closed her eyes and took a deep breath. She could smell the floral aroma from the abundance of flowers. She couldn't do anything but smile. The air blowing through her hair felt so fucking good. For a moment, she forgot about everything going bad around her.

As they approached the destination, Aries was stunned by the view.

"Is dis your place?" Aries asked as Saint slowed his truck.

"Yeah, this it. How you like it?" Saint asked as he made a complete stop and threw the truck in park.

"It's beautiful," Aries responded as she was mesmerized by what she saw. A beautiful floating hut. The roof was covered with straws and two hammocks were outside of it just above the water. Mesh net was around the place to keep bugs out. It sat right on the middle of a small manmade lake. A wooden deck and walkway led to a dock so a boat could gain access to the property.

"Yea, it's a place I come to relax and get away sometimes," he said as he reached out his hand for her. Aries paused and looked at his open palm. She smiled and looked at him with her welcoming eyes.

"Come on." She then placed her hand in his and he led her to the edge of the water where there was a small boat. It was bound by a rope, which was wrapped around a nearby tree. Aries watched as Saint released her hand and undid the rope. He then pulled the old, raggedy boat to the water and looked back at Aries.

"Let's go."

Aries loved the way Saint demanded her to come to him. She felt his power, which he never flexed. That made him even more attractive in Aries' eyes. In that moment, Aries could see herself dealing with him. She felt her button below thump and a tingle went up her spine.

"Okay…" Aries said as she laid her hand on her chest playfully, making them both smile at one another. He helped her onto the boat. He gave it a light nudge, pushing it into the water and then he quickly climbed in. He grabbed the paddle that laid on the floor.

"Dis is impressive. How long have yu've had dis?" Aries asked.

"For a few years now. I bought it to get away. I love the water and the fact that there's no neighbors. Just feels disconnected, you know. Off the grid."

"How many people know about dis spot?" Aries asked as she looked around and noticed that there weren't any other houses in sight. Matter of fact, there was nothing around except the blue water and the house.

"No one. Not even Lovey. I always wanted a place where I could go and no one could find me.

My life always moved fast so this is my way of forcing myself to slow down. Unplug," he explained.

"That sounds so relaxing. Sometimes it hard to block out all de' noise," Aries admitted.

"Exactly," Saint agreed, as he slowly dipped the paddle in the water and rowed. He switched from left to right, slowly propelling the boat to the house's dock. Once they reached it, Saint got out first and then helped her up. There was a wicker basket on the walkway and Saint picked it up. With his free hand, he went into his pocket and pulled out his cell phone. He placed it inside and then held the basket in the direction of Aries.

"No phones allowed inside," he said.

"Unplug," Aries said with a grin.

"Unplug," Saint repeated, affirming her.

He led the way to the bungalow. Aries admired the walkway and the sounds of the water as they approached. Saint pulled back the mesh net and held the opening open for Aries to enter. She looked around and saw multiple white colored pillows covered most of the floor. It seemed like an enormous bed of clouds on the floor. Saint took off his shoes and led the way. Aries followed suit and took off hers as well. Saint grabbed a lighter off the table that was off to the side. He walked around, lighting the wicker tiki lamps that were placed around the border of the room. A light scent began to fill the space.

"That smells good," Aries said as she closed her eyes and inhaled.

"It's lemon eucalyptus. It keeps the mosquitoes and bugs away," he answered.

"Me like this place," Aries said as she looked around.

"Yeah, this is my safe space," Saint answered. Aries was surprised because Saint wasn't exactly the earthy type. But that's what made him different. He was a layered man. He could move dope, have a deep conversation, and connect with nature. He walked towards Aries and pointed towards the back.

"The bathroom and guest room is in the back," he said.

"Ok cool," Aries said as she looked past him to the rear. "Mind if I go freshen up?" she asked.

"Of course," he said as he smiled and stepped to the side, giving her a clear path to the back. Aries walked past him, putting her hand on his chest on the way. As she walked away, Saint's eyes followed her ass. He admired her plump cheeks, that still somehow showed their shape through her sundress. Aries disappeared to the back and Saint looked down at his watch, seeing that it was approaching 9 a.m. He was expecting a motorboat to pull up at any moment.

On cue, he heard the faint sound of a revving engine, followed by water splashing sound. He grabbed his bookbag and exited. He walked out to the dock and saw two older women on a boat. They had sun-kissed, almond colored skin and were natives of the island. They were local farmers that Saint usually got food from when he visited his safe place. They also kept an eye on the place whenever he was away.

"Saint Von. Hello, my son!" One of the older ladies yelled from the watercraft.

"Hey, Saint!" The other woman said as well. Saint smiled as he walked to the edge to greet them.

"My two favorite island ladies," Saint said as he used one of his hands to block the sun from his eyes. The lady driving cut off the motor and let it drift towards Saint. Both ladies had colorful headwraps and floral island garbs that flowed freely.

"Beautiful morning, eh?"

"Yes indeed, it is," Saint responded.

One of the ladies reached into an oversized cooler and pulled out a large platter plate that had a variety of fruits neatly cut and covered by saran wrap. The presentation was beautiful. Saint received it and in return, he handed them the book bag full of money. The lady peeked in, smiled, and nodded her head humbly. They then pulled out a few satchels of their own and tossed them to Saint. Saint caught the bag and peeked in, seeing an abundance of pills. His monthly order was fresh from the distributor by the way of his caterers. He got on his knees, leaned down, and kissed them both on the cheek. He saw them off as they started the boat and pulled off. He made his way back to his safe haven and tossed the bags in the corner. He walked back onto the deck and slid his hands in his shorts while taking in the scenery. He then saw Aries coming out of the restroom. She had on a sheer cover-up with nothing underneath. Aries wasn't trying to be seductive; she was just comfortable in her own skin and believed that a woman should ALWAYS feel like a woman and be proud to show her nudity in the appropriate settings. This was one of those times. Saint, on the other hand, was instantly turned on.

"Wow," he said calmly as she walked onto the deck and approached him.

"Yu' like?" Aries said as she smiled and playfully spun around.

"Hell yeah," he said as he looked her up and down, running his tongue across his top lip, moisturizing them. Aries walked up to him and pinched his beard.

"Me love your teeth," Aries said.

"Yeah?" Saint said, smiling.

Aries stared at him for a brief second and released his beard. She walked over to the edge of the dock and looked around, admiring the scenery. She had never seen anything so beautiful. The green was so green and the colors were so... colored. It was breathtaking.

"Hey, me noticed dere' was no bathroom. Where it's at? I have to tinkle," she asked as she looked back at Saint.

"That's the thing. The bathroom... you are looking at it," Saint said as he looked outward.

"Wait... what?" Aries said as she blinked hard. She smiled and jerked her head back.

"Jump in..." he replied as he threw his head in the direction of the body of water.

Aries paused and thought about what he was suggesting. At first, she was about to get on her bougie shit, but then she said fuck it. It kind of felt liberating... it felt natural.

"A'ight," she said as she took the cover-up off her body.

She sat at the edge of the deck and slid in. She dipped under the water and felt free swimming in the warm pool of bliss. She opened her eyes under the water. She was in awe at the greenish-blue hue. It was so clear and it felt serene. She released herself and paddled herself above water. She shook her head and wiped the water from her eyes. She looked at Saint as he stood there, staring at her in admiration.

She swam to the deck resting her arms on the deck, holding herself up.

"Come on. Get in," she said. Saint nodded his head in agreement and began to pull off his clothes. He stripped down to his boxer briefs and walked to the deck as he stood above her.

"Jump," said Aries.

"A'ight, love," Saint said as he scanned the water.

"Come on, negro."

"Chill, I'm trying to find a spot where you didn't pee at," Saint said before he gave her a chuckle.

"Fuck yu'," Aries said playfully as she stuck her tongue out and held up her middle finger. With that, Saint jumped in and plunged into the lake. Saint dipped low and a few seconds later, he emerged from the water. Aries looked at him and admired his shiny bald head. His thick beard was wet and showing its soft texture as water dripped from it. He swam over to Aries as she held onto the deck. He used one arm to hold himself up as well. They both were now facing one another.

"I'm glad you came here with me," he said.

"Me too," she said as they stared into each other's eyes. Saint inched in closer and now they were nose to nose. She slightly turned his head and leaned forward so that his lips were right near her ear lobes.

"I want you," he whispered.

"Take me then," she answered.

Saint lined his lips up with hers and kissed her softly. First, it was a few pecks on her lips, then he reached back and palmed her ass, pulling her closer to him. The slow pecks turned into him sliding his tongue into her mouth. He began to kiss her passionately, slowly swirling his tongue around hers. Aries instantly got aroused and her nipples became erect. She reached down and felt Saint's package and she wasn't impressed. He had a short, fat manhood. However, her opinion began to change after a few tugs and it grew in the palm of her hand. She instantly knew that he was a grower and not a shower. That was the best kind. His thick pole was right above his big balls and Aries was loving what she was feeling.

They continued kissing and she stroked him slowly under the water until he was rock hard. His well-endowed penis was the thickest Aries had ever held. She grew excited, thinking about the way he was going to fill her space. Saint's lips moved from her lips, down to her breast as he latched onto her right nipple. He slowly flicked his tongue across her nipple repeatedly as Aries released his pole and cupped the back of his head. She began to moan because his warm tongue felt so good to her.

"Dat feels so good," she said as she threw her head back and looked to the blue skies above. Saint then picked her up and sat her on the deck. She felt the wood under her bottom and it felt so good. Saint, still in the water, parted her legs. He then propped herself on his elbow, slightly lifting his upper portion from the water, and kissed Aries' love box. He found her clitoris and softly sucked on it, bobbing his head back and forth, putting pressure on her button with each plunge. Aries gripped his head with both of her hands, pulling him into her.

"Oh me God, Saint. Yu' suck it so good. Yes… yes, daddy," Aries said, not being able to control her tongue. She had to call him his rightful title. Saint had a nice rhythm going and applied constant pressure. It was something about the sound of the water while getting pleasured that drove her crazy. Aries felt an orgasm and moved her hips, controlling his head. She was literally gripping his head in every spot as she felt herself about to release. Saint abruptly stopped.

"What de' fuck," Aries said with disappointment on her face. "I was almost there," she whined.

"I know, love. I want you to cum on my dick," Saint said as he looked up at her.

"Come here," Aries demanded as she scooted back, giving him room to get onto the deck.

Saint pulled himself up, exposing his thick erect pole. Aries looked down and immediately knew that he had the prettiest dick that she had ever seen. The thickness was unreal. It wasn't too long but just right. She placed her back on the warm wood and Saint positioned himself in between her legs. He grabbed his tool and rubbed it up and down on her clit before he eased in. He only went in a little. He felt her warmth and stickiness and closed his eyes in pleasure. He looked down at Aries, who was staring at him with those pretty eyes, and arched her back in pleasure. Saint stroked slow and shallow, preparing her for his girth.

"There you go," Saint praised as he felt her

loosening up from being tense. Saint leaned down and slowly kissed Aries. The more they kissed, the deeper he crept inside of her. Aries loved the way he took his time and at no point did she feel pain. It was all soft, slow, and passionate. Saint had slid into her, giving her everything he had. He laid in her as he kissed her neck and whispered in her ear.

"You doing so good, love," he said.

"Oh me God," Aries whispered as he held his back tightly.

"Bite me…" Saint directed. Aries did as she was told and locked down his collarbone.

"Soft," he instructed, feeling the sharp pain from her teeth. Aries eased up her nibble and did it slower. He slowly stroked as she adjusted.

"There you go," he coached, letting her know that she was doing it just right.

Aries loved his rhythm. She also loved how he was teaching her how he liked to make love. She adored his pace. His stroke was different from what she had ever had before. He didn't long stroke or pound her out. He laid in it and grinded deep, keeping that pressure on her. He had small strokes, never leaving the backroom of her womb. He stayed deep. It was driving her crazy. He moved his hips in small circles as he continued to kiss her neck passionately.

"You doing so good, baby," Saint whispered.

What Aries didn't know was that she had a praise kink, but Saint made her discover it right then and there. His words of confirmation as he made love to her, gave her a new feeling of ecstasy. He led her and she was a prisoner to his love-making power. He continued to push. in... out.

In... out

In... out

In... out

She loved the way his boss belly felt against her. She could feel his sack lightly tap her other hole with every thrust he took. Aries moved her hips as she placed her hands at his waist, pulling him deeper inside of her. He dragged his pole against her g-spot at the roof of her vagina and she felt a gigantic orgasm approaching. She breathed harder and shorter. Her panting gave him the signal that she was about to cum. That's when he talked her through her orgasm.

"There you go, love. Take your time. Don't rush it," he instructed. His affirming words were making Aries even wetter. She felt a big orgasm approaching, so she went back to the hard bite. She couldn't help it. She clenched his back tightly and let him know that she was about to explode.

"Me about to cum!" she yelled as she spread her

legs even more so he could get as deep as possible. Saint kept the same pace and continued stroking her out. What made Saint different from the typical man was he understood that when a woman told you that she was about to climax, you don't go harder or faster. He knew that you should keep doing what you were doing. Same cadence...

"Oh! Oh! Oh! Ugh," Aries grunted, releasing herself and pushing liquid out of her love box. Saint pulled out his pipe and gripped it tightly. He slapped his tip against her clitoris repeatedly, making her squirt again all over his stomach and inner thighs.

"There my baby go. Yea... push it out for daddy," Saint said as he looked down and watched the water show. He watched Aries' legs shake and her body jerked as the after-effects of her orgasm. She moaned with each twitching spasm. It had been so long since she had an orgasm from her g-spot and the release was much needed.

Saint admired Aries' body and the way that she moved beneath him. It was gratification of his work and that in itself turned him on even more. He gingerly slid his hand under the small of her back and flipped her over. Aries instantly leaned her head down, so her face touched the deck. She turned it so her cheek laid flat on the surface. She stuck her backside in the air, creating a seductive arch in her body. Saint raised up on his knees, lining his mid-section up with hers. He grabbed his thick pole and raised it so his pulsating tip was at the entrance of her womb. He closed his eyes and slid in. Aries gasped as her body tensed up and she received him. Saint grabbed his waist tightly and stroked her slowly once again.

"Saint..." she whispered as her face frowned and her mouth opened in pleasure. Saint slowly moved his body in a snake motion as he went deep and downward, dragging himself against her g-spot every time that he dove.

"You're taking me so good, baby," Saint said in a low tone. He slowly did this for fifteen minutes, nonstop and steady as he never changed his motion. He was giving Aries time to build up that tension again, only to have her explode even harder the next time around.

They made love on and off all day, frequently dipping into the lake. On that day, they bonded and started a connection that would permanently carve a spot in their hearts for one another.

Chapter Thirteen

EXIT GAME LEFT

Trey sat on the couch, receiving the blunt full of weed. He was in the trap house and over the past few months, he had gotten more comfortable with the spot and picked up some habits. The music was blaring and the trap was jumping. Cars were pulling up outside left and right and money was flowing. Jalen's jaws puffed out before he handed the smoke to his friend. The house was full and a group of Crows were shooting dice, while some of the others were drinking and smoking.

"Sparkle, lemme see something," Jalen said as he grabbed his crotch. Sparkle was standing over the fellas as they were shooting dice. A couple other girls were around as well and they cheered her own.

"Aye! Shake that shit, girl," one of the other girls said as she began to clap to the rhythm of afro-beat music.

Sparkle obliged with no problem and walked over to Jalen and Trey. She wanted to give them a show, up close and personal. She bent over in front of them and began to move her butt cheeks up and down, using stellar muscle control. Her gigantic rear end was shaking and it jiggled wildly as she twerked on beat. The girls in the room motivated her as they crowded around her and smacked her ass. By then, all eyes were on Sparkle and it got Chubbs' attention.

He left the dice game and walked over so he could get a better view. He had money in his hand from the game and peeled off a few twenties and sprinkled some onto Sparkle's ass, making her twerk even harder than before. This prompted a few more girls to start dancing as well. Now it was a mini strip club and four asses were flying everywhere as some of the Crows began to form around them.

Trey took deep pulls of the weed as he watched closely. Sparkle looked back and locked eyes with him, giving him a look of seduction. She had taken a liking to Trey. Sparkle loved the fact that she was the one that turned him out. She had given him some pussy a few times and saw his growth while becoming more confident in himself. She felt partly responsible for that and loved that feeling. Jalen smiled at her and then blew out a thick cloud of weed smoke.

At that moment, Crow walked from downstairs and was instantly irritated. His bipolar tendencies began to rear its ugly head; he was having a bad day. He walked over to the speaker, while nobody noticed his presence. He walked to the speaker and cut the music, prompting everyone to groan and brought them to a screeching halt. Everyone looked over at the speaker and that's when they realized Crow was the one responsible for killing the vibe.

"Dis is what wrong with de' boys. Always want to party. Niggas need to tighten de' fuck up!" Crow said as he slowly walked through the crowd, parting it like the Red Sea. He made it to the middle where Sparkle and Chubbs were. He looked at the money in Chubbs' hand and instantly grew annoyed.

"Yu' fat ass need to worry about getting some paper. Instead of throwing money on ass," Crow said as he stood face to face with Chubbs with a scowl on his face. Crow never liked Chubbs too much and after Saint told him what he tried to do to Flower, he had been looking for a reason to punish him.

"We was just having a lil fun, bro," Chubbs said

as he avoided looking Crow in the eyes.

Crow didn't respond; he just stared at him with disgust. Crow mustard up all the spit he could and spat on Chubbs, causing everyone to gasp and some people even laughed.

"Come on, Crow. Don't do the lil' nigga like that," one of the Crows said. Crow quickly looked back with a deathly stare and responded.

"Shut de' fuck up."

Crow focused back on Chubbs, who was wiping the spit away and had a look of embarrassment on his face. Crow didn't feel that was enough, so he cocked his hand back and smacked the shit out of Chubbs.

"Oh shit!" Someone yelled as he held his fist to his mouth. This prompted more people to laugh at Chubbs, while he stood there looking dumb. Chubbs nodded his head up and down and finally looked Crow in the eyes.

"A'ight bet," he said, looking like he was about to cry. Crow laughed and didn't pay Chubbs any mind. Chubbs turned around and pushed through the crowd and left the trap. He was embarrassed so badly he promised himself that he would never return to the trap again.

Crow focused his attention on his brother, Jalen, and nodded his head in the direction of upstairs. Jalen, without hesitation, followed Crow as he returned to the money run. Jalen entered just behind Crow and like usual, Lil Jupe was in there alone, sitting in the windowsill monitoring the block.

"Yu' ready to earn yo' stripes?" Crow said as he sat in the chair in the corner of the room.

"Hell yeah," Jalen answered as he rubbed his hands together. He had been waiting for Crow to say that to him for years.

"Bet, me need yu' to ride with Jupe tonight. Me got a lil issue me need taken care of," Crowd said.

"Okay, whatever it is. I'm down.

"Indeed, yu' to put in that work," Crow said as he pulled a shoebox lid from under the seat and began to roll up the weed that was inside of it.

"I'm ready," Jalen said, not being able to hold his excitement.

"A'ight bet. Me want yu' to roll out with Jupe tonight and take care of some business with that nigga that's been trying to make money on our territory. Jupe knows de' whole play. Just need yu' to follow his lead. Me need y'all lil niggas to do it because everyone in town knows the Crows. Me need some new faces to get up and close on dis' nigga," Crow instructed.

"Say less," Jalen answered simply. Just as he finished his sentence, the sound of a knock at the door filled the room. Crow frowned and eased towards the door. He slid his gun off his waist and approached the entrance with the gun in his hand. He went to the door and opened it quickly, ready to shoot.

"Put that mu'fucka up," Saint said as he stood on the last step, entering the money room. Crow's mood lightened up as he put his weapon away. Saint walked in and looked around the room. When he saw Jalen, he instantly looked at Crow like he had two heads.

"Nobody supposed to be in here, my nigga. What type of time you on?" Saint said with irritation in his voice.

"Dis me lil bro—" Crow started to say. However, Saint cut him off mid-sentence.

"Look, I don't give a fuck who this lil nigga is. Nobody suppose to be around the money except you and Jupe," Saint said as he pointed at Crow and then Jupe. Saint reached out his hand to give Jupe a handshake. Saint knew that Crow was behind the slip-up, so he didn't hold his little man accountable. Jupe was his favorite soldier because he was a boss in the making. Saint knew it was only a matter of time.

"Leave," Crow said as he never looked away from Saint. Jalen immediately exited and left the three of them in the room alone. Saint followed him and locked the door behind him.

"What's the count?" Saint asked as he threw the duffle bag he had on the floor. Jupe went to the money and filled the bag.

"We on point. But to be honest, we need to shut this bitch down. Move niggas to de' warehouse and put more focus on export and wholesale. Diaz got that operation booming," Crow suggested.

"Nigga, fuck Diaz. We need to not forget what started the shit. Our operation is our bread and butter. If we put all our eggs in Diaz's basket, he could pull everything from underneath us at any time. We have to keep our main thing our main thing, feel me?"

"Dat bitch got yu' not thinking right," Crow said. He was getting irritated by Saint's unwillingness to expand. He noticed that Saint didn't care for Diaz. But Crow saw Diaz as the pathway to become larger than life in the drug game.

"Watch yo' mouth, my nigga," Saint said as he stepped closer to Crow. He had grown close to Aries and didn't appreciate what Crow had said about her.

"Me just saying. Yu' not de' same."

"Remember who put you on. You would still be sticking up tourists and selling bullshit ass weed if it wasn't for me."

Saint's words hit Crow's ego hard and at that point, he knew that he wouldn't be Saint's lieutenant for much longer. It took everything in him not to speak his mind and tell Saint how he really felt. He decided to remain calm and hold his tongue. Although Crow was a hot head, he knew that Saint was a very dangerous man and he had an army back in the States. Crow had to be more strategic in his responses.

"Okay, boss. Yu' got it," Crow said as he walked over and helped Jupe stuff the bag. Saint was already two steps ahead of Crow and saw the look in his eyes. He knew deception was in the near future. He was nearing his exit out of the game, so he had to play mental chess with his understudy so he could transition out of the game smoothly.

"That's right, lil nigga. You been talking real slick lately. You should be more careful," Saint said sternly. Crow handed him the bag full of money. With that, Saint walked out and didn't feel good about what he was doing anymore. He was above hustling in his opinion.

Saint had a feeling of complacency. He was over selling drugs and having a person over him. He didn't like the fact that Diaz was in the picture. He told himself right then and there that he would start plotting his exit for good.

Chapter Fourteen

FORBIDDEN BLACK FRUIT

Diaz walked through the halls of the resort with his hands slid into his pocket. His white suit with thin blue pinstripes fit perfectly on his body— Italian cut of course. The smell of fresh paint filled the air and the newly marbled floor shined like a new nickel. A young lady with flowing black hair and the same eyes as Diaz was with him. It was his daughter, Christina Diaz.

"I'm so proud of you. Look at my baby. Such a great badge of honor to have a daughter like you. A bachelor's degree in business administration," Diaz said as he stopped and turned to her. He cupped her face with his hands and smiled.

It was the eve of the grand opening. He had been renovating the old resort for six months. He had renamed it, The Christina, after his daughter. Diaz had established himself on the island and it would be his hub for his criminal enterprise. He had even purchased an old automotive plant and converted it into a drug manufacturing hub. He disguised it under a toilet paper factory and had a smooth operation in place. All things led up to the event that was only twenty-four hours away.

"You will be a great general manager for this place. I personally made sure everything is in place for your success. This will be the talk of the islands for years to come."

"Thank you, Papa," Christina said as she gave him a big smile. She was a beautiful, young lady with jet black hair and a slim frame. She had big, brown eyes and an innocent appearance. She was Diaz's only child and the apple of his eye. She had just graduated from an Ivy League school back in the States. She was bright eyed and bushy tailed, loving the new task ahead of her. She had just arrived at the island and was just in time for the ribbon-cutting ceremony.

Before Diaz could say anything else to her, a group of men with a white man was leading the way. A group of about five island boys were listening attentively to their guide. The middle-aged man held a clipboard in his hand as he pointed around and talked to the young men. He looked over and perked up when he saw Diaz. The man walked towards Diaz with a smile.

"Hello, boss," the man said as he extended his hand while approaching.

"Oh, Tom," Diaz said as he shook his hand. He looked over at Christina as they shook hands. "Great that I caught you. I want to introduce you to the star of the show. This is my daughter, Christina Diaz," he said proudly. Tom instantly focused his attention on her and reached out his hand.

"Ms. Diaz! I heard so much about you. It's my pleasure to meet you," he said, full of enthusiasm.

"Hello. The pleasure is mine," she said humbly as she shook his hand.

"Tom is our head of security and valet," Diaz said.

"Yes, I'm going to make sure this is a smooth experience for all of our guests. Security and great service is my top priority. Anything you need, I'm your guy. I'm training our security staff as we speak. They're all locals and eager to learn quickly," he said as he looked back at the group of young men. Crow was amongst the group. Saint had sent him to apply for the position along with his members so they would have an inside edge on the resort. Most of their clientele were tourists and what better place to service them than through the newest resort on the island.

Diaz smiled and placed his hand on Tom's shoulder.

"I need to have a moment with you," he requested.

He wanted to quickly speak with him about the expectations he had for Tom's position. He briefly left his daughter alone and it wasn't long before her attention focused on Crow. His distinct look intrigued her and she instantly got turned on. She looked towards his crotch and wondered what he looked like naked. She had a secret fetish for black men and their tools. She found out quickly that the myths were true about the endowment difference in black men versus any other race. She liked dark men and Crow was hands down the darkest man she had ever seen. She instantly wanted him as a trophy and another notch under her belt.

The other boys weren't paying her any mind and talked amongst each other, looking at the spacious lobby and new look. Everyone except Crow. His eyes were on Christina. He stared at her without reservation or discreetness. He was fearless and he didn't give a fuck if Diaz or Tom saw him. That alone turned Christina on. He was a beast and she loved that kind. Crow smiled slightly, showing off his gold teeth and Christina smiled back. She took a glance over at her father and Tom and noticed that they were too deep into their conversation to pay attention to her. So, in return, she focused back on Crow.

She discreetly squirmed and crossed her legs, squeezing her thighs together. She tried to vaguely scratch the sexual itch that she was beginning to have below. Diaz never had an idea that his baby girl was a nympho; however, Crow caught on instantly. He wore linen slacks, so he followed her eyes and knew what she was searching for, so he gave it to her. He slid his hands in his pocket and slightly pulled his pants towards himself, so his print could show better. Christina gasped and put her hand on her chest, unable to control her excitement. In her peripheral view, she saw her father and Tom heading back her way and quickly looked at them, smiling.

"Come on, sweetheart," Diaz said and he placed his hand on her back. "Let's check out the rest of the place and let Tom get back to work."

Diaz led his daughter away, but not before she looked at Crow and he threw his head in the direction of the pool area on the opposite side of the lobby. With that, she left with her father. However, she wasn't thinking about anything but getting to that pool area to see what Crow had in mind.

***

"You have a call from an inmate at Jackson federal penitentiary. To accept the call, please press 5…"

Aries took the phone from her ear and looked down at it. She pressed the dial and waited for the inmate to connect.

"Hey, Mika," the voice said on the opposite end. Aries smiled when she heard Miamor's voice. It had been a while since she heard from her so it warmed her heart. Aries always laughed when Miamor called her different made-up names, not wanting to call her Aries on a recorded line.

"Hey, bitch," Aries said, sending them both into laughter. "Me miss yu', gyal," Aries added.

"I miss you too, hoe," Miamor said.

"So what's been going on? I'm so ready to get out this place."

"Me too! Me so glad you'll be home and out of that hell hole."

"Tell me about it. The only thing Trump did good was pass that bill."

"Yu' can say that again," Aries responded.

"Yea… so what's been up with you? You been missing my calls… you must be getting some dick."

"Gyal…" Aries said, smiling from ear to ear.

"I knew it. I can hear it in your voice. So come on, tell me about this guy. What's his name? He from the town?" Miamor asked, referring to Miami.

"Nah. Yu' know better than that," Aries replied.

"I see. I can't wait to see you, Mika. For real. I get out this bitch in one more month. I swear, I'm never trying to see this place again. I miss my baby," Miamor said, referring to her son.

"How is CJ?" Aries asked, smiling thinking about her nephew.

"He's a grown ass man. He looks exactly like Carter. It's spooky how much they resemble."

"Me haven't seen him in years. Me used to see him on TV all de' time when he was boxing, yu' know?"

"Yeah, well those days are gone. I wish he still was boxing, then I wouldn't have to worry about him so much," Miamor answered with obvious disappointment in her voice. Aries instantly knew what Miamor meant. CJ had followed in his parent's footsteps and was in the streets. The apple never fell too far from the tree.

"He'll be ok, me sure. Me need to send my boy with him for the summer. He needs to be around family. He's so timid, yu' know. He's a sweetheart but he's not built like that. Me boy is a softy," Aries said jokingly. She knew Trey grew up sheltered and that would only hinder him when he was older and in the real world.

"Being a softy is good. I wish we didn't grow up how we did. That street shit is overrated. You see where I'm at? It cost me my husband, my son, and my freedom. You're doing an amazing job raising him," Miamor stated.

"I hear yu,' gyal," Aries said unenthused just before she pivoted the conversation. "How long yu' got to be on papers when yu' come home?'

"Forever bitch," Miamor said, sending them both into a fit of laughter.

They caught up for the next fifteen minutes and vaguely talked in codes to each other. They were experts in talking on tapped phones. They tried to keep the communication at a minimum, but on special days they always connected.

"Somebody's birthday is tomorrow," Miamor said.

"Me getting old," Aries responded.

"You're not getting old, you're getting better. So, what're doing on your day?"

"Probably going to breakfast with baby boy and then me guy friend got something planned."

"Oooh, what ya'll got going?" Miamor asked with excitement in her voice.

"Shiddd. Me don't know. He won't tell me what it is though."

"You have one minute remaining…"

The voice of the operator interrupted their conversation, giving them both a feeling of sadness. The harsh reality had set in. It was a reminder that they were apart and one of them was locked up like an animal.

"Let me get off this before it hangs up. Enjoy your birthday and I'll see you soon."

"I love yu,' Mia!"

"I love you too, Sharon!' Miamor said, making them both laugh until the phone disconnected.

Trey listened closely as his mother spoke about him on the phone candidly with his auntie. He had come down the stairs and caught her conversation without her knowing. Her words hit him like a ton of bricks. Hearing his mother express her true feelings about him gave him a sense of weakness. All the wolves around him, it was hard being a lamb. The fact that his mother looked at him as a weakling gave him a feeling of emptiness.

Aries didn't notice Trey, so she went out towards the back patio, leaving him there to tend to his thoughts. Trey left the house with rage in his heart. He was going to prove to her that he wasn't a soft, little boy anymore. He was dead set on making her respect him.

***

Detective Wade sat in the back of a flower delivery truck with her small team of agents. The inside of the truck was equipped with top-of-the-line surveillance monitors and a makeshift FBI hub. They were parked just outside of the resort and close enough for them to catch the different conversations via wiretaps and hidden mics. She watched closely as the cameras showed different cameras that were placed inside of the new resort. They had infiltrated Diaz's staff and placed over a dozen of undercovers that acted as construction workers, putting the entire resort under the close watch of the FBI. They had just as many cameras installed as Diaz had.

Wade had hit the jackpot with tailing Aries. Although she couldn't catch Aries doing any recent crimes, it led her to Diaz. Diaz was also on the radar of the authorities back home and while Wade was waiting for Aries to slip up, she was subsequently building a case on Diaz and his crew... Saint included. She had gathered enough information to bring federal charges against Diaz and she had never had a better constellation prize in her entire career.

"It's almost time," Wade said as she took her headphones off, stood up, and put her hands on her hips. She had disappeared from the island's watch and the character, Flower, was dead in her eyes. She had been building a silent indictment for so long; it had become an obsession. She was set on taking down the entire island with her findings. Cases like this catapulted agents to heights that were legendary. By her being from a law enforcement family, she knew that this move would bring honor and prestige to her family's name. She was focused. Wade wanted blood. She glanced at one of the monitors that were placed inside one of the pools looming lights.

"Aye. Zoom in on camera five," she said as she squinted her eyes and leaned in towards the screen. One of the agents pushed a few buttons on his laptop and the small square on the screen expanded. Now Wade could see the footage crystal clear.

"Crow," Wade said under her breath as all her attention was on the man walking across the screen, looking suspicious. Crow was looking around, obviously trying to make sure no one was watching him. Wade focused on him attentively, trying to figure out what was he up to. She was to see him at the facility. She knew what connected him to Saint, but the connection to Diaz had her perplexed.

At that point, all the agents' attention was on the screen, trying to see what was going on. Just as everyone's eyes were glued to the screen, a woman appeared in the same area. Wade instantly noticed the woman and turned her head to the side. It was Christina; Diaz's daughter. She had been on Wade's radar for a few months since she had been visiting the island to see her dad. With all of Christina's academic accolades, she knew that she wouldn't take long to join the family business. They all watched in confusion, but things became clearer when they witnessed Crow and Christina disappear into a utility closet.

***

"Yu' like black dick, eh?" Crow said as he hastily pulled down his pants. He pulled down the front of his boxer brief and exposed himself. Christina's eyes got big and her mouth began to water as she looked at his long, low hanging pole. She instantly was turned on as she admired how dark and long it was. Even with him not being erect, he still was bigger than her fiancé at his best. She dropped to her knees, grabbed Crow's manhood, and examined it like a prized possession.

"Eat that mu'fucka," Crow demanded as he palmed the back of her head. She did as she was told and wrapped her mouth around him, taking him all. Crow looked down at her as he aggressively gripped her hair and tried his best to jam himself as far as he could into the back of her throat. She gagged repeatedly but never stopped giving him fellatio.

Gawk!

Gawk!

Gawk!

The more she sucked, the more forceful Crow got with her. He had gotten fully erect and began to thrust himself into her. He used the back of her throat as a punching bag for his pole. He was impressed by her lack of gag reflexes. His brow sweated as he continued to pump her face.

"Yu' swallow all of dis. Every drop," he demanded as he felt himself about to explode.

"No… hold on," Christina said as she paused and quickly unbuttoned her shirt, exposing her bra. She was soaking wet below and she wanted to feel Crow. But Crow had other plans as he began to stroke himself with his free hand. With his free hand, he yanked Christina's hair back and began to release himself over her face.

"Ugh!" he grunted and he shook violently as he painted her chin and neck area with his nectar.

"Why didn't you hold it? I wanted you to fuck me hard. I want you right now," Christina said, breathing rapidly, lusting for the forbidden fruit in front of her. She stood up and lifted her skirt; however, Crow was jiggling his pole and shaking away what he had left onto the floor.

"No, I got shit to do," Crow said coldly. He encountered tourists all the time that had fetishes for dark, black men, so this wasn't anything new to him. In fact, older women would travel there just for that reason alone and he frequently took advantage of their desires.

"Please, come on. Put it in," Christina begged with no shame. Her disease of addiction was on full display and she couldn't help it as she rubbed herself with a crazed look in her eyes.

"No bitch. Come to Jimmy's and I'll give yu' exactly what yu' want," he said as he reached down and felt her wetness. He slipped his finger inside of her and slowly pulled it out, rubbing across her clitoris. Christina's body trembled and she grabbed his arm and closed her eyes. He repeated that motion four times and leaned in and whispered.

"Jimmy's on Friday night just before midnight. Yu' hear me, bitch?" said Crow.

"Yes. Yes, daddy I hear you," Christina said as she squirmed and humped against his finger. Crow slid his soaked finger out of her and placed it in her mouth. She sucked his two fingers clean and with that, Crow left her there with a wet ass and a thirst to feel him.

***

Saint and Aries were at Saint's house on the lake laying on the pillows, enjoying the view. Saint's safe haven had quickly become Aries' as well. That's where they would go and connect. Over the time that they had been together, it was special. They spent almost every day together and they were connected mentally and physically. Their thought-provoking conversations always held weight. Aries had never met a man that was smart enough to have high-level talks while being dangerous. She loved a man that was cutthroat with the world while being gentle with her. Saint was the best of both worlds and a man's man. He wasn't perfect by far, but he was perfect for her.

Aries smoked a joint while she laid in Saint's lap.

"So, yu' really getting out dis' shit, huh?" Aries asked as she looked up at him and passed him the weed. He received it, took a long drag, and inhaled.

"Yeah, it's time. I ran all my dirty money through that mu'fucka. I have enough to live comfortably for the rest of my life. At this point, I'm just doing it because that's what I'm used to," Saint said.

"Yu' know what? Me been feeling de' same way. Me just wanna disappear, yu' know. Then me got dis' mu'fucka Diaz breathing down me back."

"Tell me about it," Saint said as he shook his head in disgust.

Diaz had snaked his way into both of their businesses and kind of had them both by the balls. They couldn't shake him without causing an uproar and potentially fucking up what they had going on.

"He just doesn't know. The old me would have him hanging by a light post for even approaching me," Aries said, shaking her head. She knew that if Diaz understood who she truly was, it would be a different story between them. He only knew a little bit about her past, but what he did know was enough to keep her cooperating with him. She couldn't risk someone blowing the whistle on her and her spending time in a U.S. prison. She had to play ball for her son.

"On another note. Yo' bitch ass goon was snooping around the restaurant de' other day," Aries said as she received the joint back from Saint.

"What you mean, love?" Saint asked as he frowned up in confusion.

"De' nigga Crow," she responded.

"What's that about? Why didn't you tell me?" Saint asked as he sat all the way up, shifting Aries so she would have to sit down as well.

"Me a big girl. Me don't have to run and tell yu' about dumb shit. Me can handle myself."

"Okay. What did he say?" Saint asked as he was noticeably irked.

"Mentioned something about me distracting yu' and I should think about breaking it off with yu'."

"Wait what? Are you serious?" Saint asked. He clenched his jaws so tight that the muscles in his temple began to flex. He was heated.

"He's a kid. That lil' nigga don't want problems with me. Trust," Aries said, knowing what she was capable of. A few calls and she could have Miami hitters on the island, shaking things up.

Saint remained silent, but his mind was racing trying to figure out what was Crow's motive. He had crossed the line by approaching Aries. Saint understood that cutting Crow off was inevitable and he planned to do that sooner rather than later. It was only a matter of time before Crow became a bigger issue and Saint was aware.

Saint looked down at Aries and admired her beauty. He quickly switched his focus to her and blocked out the negative thoughts. He would tend to that business another time.

"Sometimes, I want to stay here forever. Like away from the islands," Saint admitted.

"Right, me can understand why yu' say that."

"It's like a nigga came to the islands to get away from the bullshit. But then... the bullshit always catches up. This wasn't an escape. It was a trick bag. I just opened shop in a different country," Saint said, talking to Aries but also to himself. He shook his head as the realization hit him. He was in the black man's rat race. He took a drag of the joint and passed it back. "I got on the same shit I was running from," Saint admitted.

"Trust me. Me know exactly what yu' are saying. Past sins never stay in de' past."

"No more past talk. We're focusing on the future, right?" Saint asked as he looked down at Aries.

"Yeah. You're right. De' future sounds good," Aries responded.

"Somebody's birthday is coming," Saint said and then leaned down to kiss her forehead.

"What yu' got for me?" Aries said playfully.

"You know I'm not telling you that," Saint said

while smiling. "I just need you to meet me by the shore. Just before sunset. Can you do that for me?" Saint asked.

"Me can do that," Aries responded as she felt butterflies in the pit of her stomach. She was giddy like a little girl, thinking about what Saint had planned for them. She loved the way he focused on her and gave her his time. She loved everything about Saint. He was patient with her. He was protective while giving her space. He was a man who understood where she came from and they related on many levels. He was her safe place. He was her *saint*. She looked at him in admiration and at that moment, she knew that she was in love. This was what made her decision so hard.

Just days before, she had discovered that she was pregnant. After taking three tests, she was sure that she had a bean in the oven. She looked at Saint and knew that he would make a great father. His instinct to protect and provide was something that made him a perfect candidate. She told herself that she would decide to tell him or not by the end of the week. She battled herself within her thoughts and began to think about the possibilities. One of them was the thought of getting caught by the authorities because of her past life as a Murder Mama. She kept envisioning having a baby in jail.

That thought alone made abortion an option. She would make her decision after her birthday. Also, Miamor had just come home and she would confide in her to help with her final call.

Chapter Fifteen

HUSTLER'S AMBITION

Mounds of powdered fentanyl was on the table along with a variety of illegal pharmaceuticals. Over the past few months, business had exploded and that came directly from Diaz's partnership and expansion. His widespread demand over the southern region, mixed with the production speed, made for a perfect marriage between he and Saint. The pipeline that they had created was running smoothly and Diaz's plans were working just as designed.

Crow walked up and down the rows of the new and spacious warehouse. He was overseeing the dozen females who were counting the pills, bottling them up, and prepping them for distribution. His eyes were busy, moving right to left, left to right. He was like a keen hound dog, on top of everything moving. There was a round table dedicated to mixing small amounts of fentanyl with the other powder drugs. They were using machines to mold them into pill form, giving them more potency, which made them more effective.

As usual, he was making sure that no one got sticky fingers with the product. He loved the new warehouse and shit was moving. Diaz took them to a whole new level and they were able to move the pills outside of the island. They had penetrated Florida and flooded their streets with a variety of pills. Crow looked around and felt a euphoric feeling of power. All his Crows were spread around with semi-automatic weapons, ready to pop off at his command. He looked over at Luis, who was playing a game on his phone, completely oblivious to what was going on around him. Crow shook his head in disgust as he resented the fact that he was in a position of power and literally did nothing but sit around on his phone all day. Crow's attention was so focused on the operation, he didn't notice Diaz and his three henchmen walk in.

Diaz wore his signature white suit as he casually walked in, leading his pack. Two buff security goons were right on his heels. Luis did notice his uncle enter. He quickly stood up and put away his phone. He swiftly headed in his uncle's direction with a nervous demeanor. Luis wanted his uncle to think he was in charge and supervising operations as he was instructed to do. To be honest, Luis did nothing to contribute to the business and his arrogant sense of entitlement rubbed everyone the wrong way.

"Hey, Uncle. What are you doing here?" Luis asked with a forced smile.

"Never mind the reason. How's everything moving?" Diaz asked.

"Uh yeah... we are on schedule and shits getting done," Luis replied.

"Good. I have a large order from the Midwest we need to fill. How many bars can we have by Sunday?" Diaz inquired.

"Uh..." Luis stumbled as he looked back at the workers. It was obvious that he didn't know the answer to his uncle's question; the confusion was written all over his face.

"We can have ten dimes," Crow interjected as he stood a few feet away. Ten dimes were slang for ten thousand units. Luis looked over at Crow and brushed past his incapable nephew.

"Are you sure about that?" Luis asked as he walked to Crow. Crow nodded his head, confirming that they could.

"That's great news. By Sunday, correct?"

"By Sunday," Crow said in a low tone.

Crow looked Diaz directly in his eyes without blinking, showing no fear or uncomfortableness. He was confident that the order could be filled. Luis and Crow stood there for a minute, creating an awkward silence. Luis was reading him and he liked what he was seeing. Crow didn't give a fuck and it showed.

"I've been eyeing you around here when I check-in. You keep this place running, I see. What's your name?" Luis asked just after he broke the staring contest. He cracked a slight smile as he slickly slipped his hands into his slacks and shifted his weight from one side to the other.

"Crow," he responded.

"Yeah, that's it. Crow," Luis said as he looked around as if he was jogging his memory. He continued. "Where is Saint?" he asked.

"He's not here today," Crow answered as he slightly hovered over Diaz.

"When is the last time he's been here?" Diaz asked as he seemed to become more interested.

"Few weeks maybe," Crow replied.

"Is that right?"

"Saint is so far up de' island gyal ass, he can't see straight," Crow said before smiling and showing a glimpse of his gold teeth. They both shared a laugh and Diaz placed his hand on Crow's shoulder. Crow instantly got on defense and looked at Diaz's hand. His body tensed up and he was ready to take it wherever Diaz was.

"Calm down, son," Diaz said as he felt the tension. "Give me a tour of this place," Diaz said, being that he had never visited the warehouse before. Diaz turned to his goons and put his hand up, palm facing them.

"It's ok... it's ok," Diaz said, signaling them to let them walk alone. Both of the henchmen nodded their heads, understanding their boss' request.

"Come on.... show me what's making me rich," Diaz said jokingly. He turned Crow around and nudged him to start walking.

"So, I know my incompetent nephew isn't helping much. But I promised my brother, his father, that I would look after him before he died. I had to introduce him to the family business to keep him from doing something stupid. You must keep someone like him busy, ya know?"

"Understood," Crow said as it began to make more sense to him. He always wondered why Saint insisted on Luis to work with them.

They walked in between the rows of tables as the workers did their part of the operation. Everything was clicking on all cylinders. The sound of the liftgate echoed through the facility and trucks began to pull in backwards, preparing for loading as the pills were packaged and hidden in produce on their way to Florida for distribution. Everyone had on a mask and was shirtless. Everyone's hands were moving and it was a beautiful sight to see. Diaz was impressed. Crow explained every aspect to him as they observed the mechanics of what was becoming the hub of one of the biggest opioid distribution centers in the entire Caribbeans.

Diaz watched and listened closely as Crow knowledgeably broke down everything from A to Z. They made their way to the second level, where the office was at. They could look down and see the main floor through a wide glass.

Diaz slid his hands into his pocket and nodded his head in satisfaction. He turned to Crow, who was intently looking at the workers, making sure no one attempted to steal.

"Let me ask you this, son. Could you run this, without Saint?" Diaz asked as he looked directly at Crow. Diaz wasn't sure what Crow would say. Would he grow offended and tell Saint? Or would he use this opportunity to move up the ladder of his criminal enterprise?

Crow returned the gaze and looked to see if he was being tested. He wondered was Diaz testing his loyalty to Saint. Crow wasn't from an affluent family. Crow had never been anyone's favorite. He looked at Diaz's question as an offering from God. All street niggas prayed to get next to the plug. This all went through Crow's mind in a split second and then he spoke.

"Me could. Dis comes natural to me," Crow responded.

"Whatdoes Saint do exactly?"

Crow stopped walking and looked at Diaz directly in his eyes. He remained silent and that taciturnity told Diaz everything he needed to know. Crow gave him a gaze that said, *"Me... I'm the captain of this ship."* He slightly stuck out his chest and clenched his teeth tightly, showing Diaz the muscles in his jawbone. Diaz paused and stared at Crow. He was fascinated. Crow had the eye of the tiger. Crow was also a town native and through Diaz's experiences, he understood the upside to being of the community. The amount of drugs that they were pushing, they needed the island to know and understand the concept of omerta. A successful trafficker had to be a street version of a politician. He decided at that moment to mold Crow into that.

"What are you doing Friday?" asked Diaz.

"What do me need to be doing?" Crow asked, knowing what time it was.

"Good. I'll send a car for you Friday evening."

"I'll be on de' block. Yu' need an address, eh?" Crow asked.

"I know exactly where it is," Diaz said with a smile. He placed a hand on his shoulder and leaned forward in an endearing manner. Diaz then turned and returned in the direction of his henchmen and walked past them towards the door. Without saying a word, his men followed him out, and just like that… they were out of the door.

***

Saint walked along the beach, holding Aries' hand. It was exactly a year to the day that he had first made love to her. So, he asked her to accompany him for a night. He asked her to wear white. That was his only request. Saint wore white too. She had a blindfold on and the sand under her feet told her they were at the beach.

"What's going on? Where are we doing, eh?" Aries asked with the biggest smile on her face. She couldn't stop smiling, feeling the anxiety in her chest. Good anxiety. He timed the rendezvous to happen at 6:37 p.m. Saint held her hand tightly as he looked over at her. He couldn't help but to smile as well. Her energy was that of pure joy and her aura was pure. Scientists called it energy, hippies call it aura, but their culture called it vibes. The vibe was right and the night was just right.

"Don't worry about it, love. We almost there, love. I got you," Saint assured her as he wrapped his arm around her waist, carefully guiding her.

"Yu' are crazy," she said as she thought about not knowing what's going on. She was nervous and excited at the same time. She couldn't believe that she allowed a man to blindfold her, totally letting her guard down. She was trusting a man. This was when she realized that she really loved the man by her side. She trusted him. That was something she could honestly admit that she never had with a man.

The sounds of the ocean were the soundtrack playing in the background. Saint came to a stop and Aries followed suit as she let out a light giggle, excited in anticipation.

"Pretty girl... thanks for being you," Saint whispered as he held her from the back and buried his head between her neck and collarbone.

He gently kissed it, sending a tingling feeling up Aries' spine. Aries still had her eyes closed and smiled as she reached around and gently grabbed the back of Saint's neck. Aries threw her head back in pleasure and giggled. She then bit her bottom lip, feeling herself getting aroused. Her nipples began to harden and stuck out, fully erect. She finally looked in front of her where the light music was coming from and she expected a candlelight dinner or something of that nature, but Saint had something else up his sleeve.

What she saw blew her mind and left her stuck. She didn't know how to feel when she saw the surprise Saint had for her. It was a small area covered in red rose petals, just far enough from the waves so they wouldn't wash away. It was a small speaker playing the subtle island music and a massage table on the rose petals. She saw two completely naked women rubbing oil on one another. They both had sun kissed skin that glowed in the moonlight. They were rubbing each other's breasts and asses as they passionately kissed and squirmed in pleasure.

As Aries looked deeper, she saw that it was the red hair girl that they had met at the bar a while back. Aries' eyes drifted to Red's big, round behind. Her ass cheeks looked even better without clothing. The two, big bubbles that Red had behind her jiggled every time she moved. Red lowered her head and started to suck on the nipples of the Latino woman. The Latino woman had a slim build and a small bubble that poked out behind her. Her breast was big and perky with nipples that sat on oversized dark areolas. Red gripped one of her breasts and squeezed it, taking it into her mouth.

Red looked at Aries as she slowly ran her tongue in a circular motion around the other woman's nipple. Red then dropped her free hand and began to tease herself, rubbing her completely bald love box. Aries couldn't help but notice Red's fat lips below. They looked swollen and they were slightly hanging down. Aries looked back at Saint and then to the girls again, not fully understanding what was going on.

"Saint. What we doing, eh?" Aries asked with confusion written all over her face.

"Just relax. It's your night," Saint said as he gently grabbed her hand and led her towards the action. In Aries' mind, she wanted to pull away, but her body was telling her something different and she followed without hesitation. Aries had thought about Red a few times since the day they had met, but she never would of imagined seeing her again in this capacity. A sense of euphoria overcame her as Saint led her to the other two women.

Red took her attention from the Latino girl and focused solely on Aries as they approached. Red ran her tongue over her top lip and groped her own breast, then pinched her nipple. She too had wanted Aries for quite some time. Saint guided

Aries' hand towards them and Aries' hand inside of Red's. It was as if they were passing a baton in a relay race. Aries wanted to contest but the pulsation in her clitoris prevented her from saying anything. She looked back at Saint, who was watching closely as he took a cigar out of his pocket and lit it. He then walked to the side where a chair was waiting. He sat and watched as his birthday present for Aries unfolded.

Aries' eyes followed him as she looked for answers. She was puzzled but for some reason, a smile formed on her face and it was as if his was contagious. Red gently removed the dress by pulling the strings from Aries' shoulders. Aries looked down as her dress dropped. She stood there naked. Saint requested her to not wear panties. Aries rarely was shaken or nervous but her heart was pounding because she had never been in that position with a woman before. Red grabbed her hand again and then led her to the massage table. She laid Aries down tenderly. Red put her full lips right on Aries' earlobes.

"Happy Birthday," she whispered.

The Latino girl reached down and grabbed a bottle. She poured coconut oil on Aries' inner thigh. She then gently rubbed while passing the bottle to Red. Red poured some on Aries' breast.

Aries looked over at Saint as he watched intensely while blowing his weed. She could see his print through his linen pants and that turned her on even more. He pulled out his slightly erect pole and laid it just over his beltline. Aries was turned on even more as she saw his thick dick sitting there and slightly jumping. It seemed like every time it jumped, she could feel her clitoris pulsate. Aries' mind was blown. She wanted to sit on Saint so bad and ride his well-endowed manhood. Aries smiled at Saint once again and then felt a tongue on her stomach.

She turned her head and looked down as Red stared at her. Red slowly licked a trail and ended up at Aries' nipple. Red circled her nipple and moaned, making Aries squirm at the sight. Moments later, Aries felt two hands gently spreading her thighs. The Latino girl began massaging her inner thigh and the sides just outside her vagina. Aries felt herself getting wet as she clenched her butt cheeks, making blood circulate to her vagina as her clitoris began to slightly poke out from her yoni's lips. She closed her eyes and enjoyed her full body massage. The Latino girl worked the waste down as Red massaged her upper portion. They both massaged very slowly and took their time. This drove Aries crazy as she enjoyed the tantric experience.

The sound of the waves and island music relaxed her as they rubbed her entire body in unison. Red then asked Aries to flip over. Aries, in a trance, submitted to Red's request. Now her cheeks were laying on the table and she looked at Saint and noticed that he was now fully erect. Aries licked her lips, wanting him so bad.

She began to slowly hump the table, trying to get friction on her lady. Saint had put out his smoke and was slowly stroking himself while returning the gaze. Aries felt like she was in a dream. She was in complete bliss. She licked her lips and she noticed that Saint reacted instantly. She could see the vein running up the bottom of his penis and his fat ball sack hung freely.

Aries felt someone spreading her butt cheeks and a warm tongue slid into her anus, making her jump from the unexpected sensation. She looked back and saw the top of Red's head. Red began to lick up and down, running over Aries' anus with each swipe. A moan slipped from Aries' lips unintentionally. Aries saw Red's big ass th in the air as she slowly swung it side to side. Aries then noticed the Latino girl standing behind her with her face buried in between her ass. The slurping noises were like an aphrodisiac.

Aries was all in at that point; she wanted some dick. She raised her ass in the air and softly leaned into Red's face. Red began to eat Aries' love box from the back. Aries began to rock back and forth, crashing her love box into Red's tongue each time. Aries was in a full fledge threesome and she couldn't believe it. Aries sped up her pace as it began to feel good to her. She started to crash harder and harder into Red's face as she closed her eyes and bit her bottom lip. She heard Red moaning and it was driving her crazy. Aries lifted one hand and began to pinch and pull her nipple. She felt an orgasm coming and moaned even louder. Red stopped licking, not wanting Aries to cum yet. Aries turned around, wondering why she stopped. Red stood up and played with herself. The Latino girl stood behind and rubbed Red's breast as she masturbated. Red whispered to Aries.

"Turn around... lay down," she demanded, looking directly into Aries' eyes.

Aries turned around and laid on her back. Red slowly straddled Aries and lined her pussy up with Aries. She took two fingers and spread her vagina lips as she looked down to line up her clitoris. Aries instantly felt Red's hot vagina against hers. Red was so wet. Red began to grind Aries and moaned softly as her breast hung down right near Aries' face. Aries began to suck her nipples. She looked over at Saint as he was placing his pole into the mouth of the Latino girl. Just the sight drove Aries crazy. She bobbed her head up and down and made loud slurping noises as Saint threw his head back in pleasure. Aries focused back on Red and noticed her lustful eyes. Red leaned down while still grinding and began to kiss Aries. Red's pace became faster and harder as she whispered.

"Oh, my God. I'm about to cum, baby. Fuck. That pussy so good and soft," she said. Aries felt her own orgasm build up as well. Aries grabbed Red's ass and squeezed her plump, soft cheeks as she pulled Red's body closer and tighter. Aries squirmed intensely as she began to rotate her hips. Red kicked her leg over and now they were in a scissor position. Aries gasped as she began to caress her own breast. The new position allowed their clitorises to match up perfectly. Red had a huge clitoris and it felt like a penis to Aries. Up and down, circle, circle. Red was working her ass against Aries. The moaning became louder and louder. They both had an orgasm approaching.

"Damn," Aries said as she squeezed her breast even tighter. Red started grinding aggressively and their bald love boxes allowed them to feel everything. Red slightly lifted her mid-section, let out a scream, and a gush of liquid shot out of her vagina and onto Aries' pelvic area. The warm sensation sent Aries over the edge as she placed her two fingers down below to her love. She began to rub swiftly across her own button as Red was still squirting on her and jerking her body with each spray. Aries orgasmed and arched her back as she rubbed one out. It felt so euphoric to Aries. The feeling of being squirted on gave her a sensation that she had never felt before. She orgasmed harder than she ever had. The squirt landed on her as she continued to rub. Both of them screamed in pleasure together. Red dismounted Aries and wobbled a little because her legs were so weak.

By that time, Saint was walking over to the table and the Latino woman followed him. Saint was fully erect and stood over Aries as she slightly rubbed herself, coming down from the explosive orgasm. She and Saint locked eyes as he walked to the foot of the massage table near her feet. He smoothly reached behind her knees with both hands and pulled her closer to him. He placed the bottom of her feet on his chest and slightly spread her thighs. She looked down at his thickness and smiled at him. He began to stroke himself and placed his tip directly on her clit. He grabbed his pole and began massaging her clit while staring at Aries' swollen button.

He looked to the side and began to lick one of her toes, circling his tongue around it. He took his time with each lick. It was like he was tongue kissing it. Aries watched as his tongue came into view with each circle. It began to make her thump down there once again. She squirmed as the sensation of his hard penis and the visual drove her crazy. The two girls stood on each side of the table. They both took one of Aries' breasts and began to slowly suck them. All of Aries' hotspots were being stimulated simultaneously. Everyone there was solely focused on Aries' body.

This nigga is a genius, Aries thought as she realized that he put this all together.

He was the mastermind and architect. She felt like a queen. Everyone was being gentle and slow as they pleased her. They were all moving to the same drum. Aries knew that Saint had given careful instructions because that's how he made love. He always took his time and conquered the art of tantric sex.

Aries felt another orgasm building and her breathing sped up. She arched her back as she gasped. Saint stop sucking her toes and looked directly at Aries.

"Love... Love. Look at me," he instructed. Aries was almost in a trance with her eyes closed. It seemed like his voice snapped her out of it. She looked at him and they just gazed into one another's eyes.

"Happy Birthday, love," he said. He then put both of his hands on her thighs. He spread them, giving him easy access to her ocean.

"You doing so good, love," he whispered as he talked her through the sex like he always did. That was one thing Aries always loved about him; Saint always talked calmly and reassured her through sex. Just his voice made her feel safe. She loved the way he would talk her through her orgasms.

"There you go," he said as Aries spread her legs even wider for him. That's when he dropped that dick in her. She let out a moan and jumped. Saint always went deep and didn't shit change because they weren't alone. He pushed himself deep inside of Aries and let it sit in the back of her womb. He dug deep as he stood on his toes and he leaned forward so she could feel every inch of him. He laid in it and began to slowly rock inside of her. He didn't long stroke. He kept that pressure on her and stayed deep. He pulled back about an inch and then crashed back into the bottom of her box. He did that slowly and with power. She could feel his dominance with each stroke. He never sped up; he was steady and hard as a rock. He stood straight up and placed his two fingers inside of Aries' mouth. Aries sucked it, wetting his fingers up for him. He then placed those two fingers on her clit as did a combo move, stimulating the outside and the inside of her love box.

"Damn, baby, I'm so proud of you," he whispered as he slowly did his thing. Aries had a praise kink and she never knew until she met Saint. Saint kept this up for ten minutes straight, moving unhurriedly by design. The two women rotated licking Aries' breasts, kissing one another, and then eventually kissing Aries.

Aries was soaked. So soaked, the sound of her box was louder than the waves it seemed. Saint began to speed up, now pulling his pole back a little further, giving her a longer stroke. Aries felt his sack hitting her other hole with every thrust. She loved it. She felt another orgasm building up and couldn't help but to talk to Saint.

"I'm about cum, Saint. Oh me God. I'm about to cum," she said as she humped back and he stroked. Saint jerked as he felt himself about to climax as well.

"Me too, love. Me too," he whispered. At that point, she was pulling his tool back, almost taking it out with each pump. He was giving her the long stroke. And that's when it happened.

"Ohh!" Saint said as he pulled out his dick and released himself on Aries' box. Aries screamed as her body shook aggressively.

"Ohhhh! Shit, boy!" she said as she released.

They had orgasmed together and they both were smiling in pleasure. Saint stepped back and watched Aries' legs shake. That's when the Latino came around the table and took Saint's place at the end of the table. She bent down and began to lick Saint's cum off Aries' box. She then began to suck on Aries' clit. It felt so good to Aries because she sucked pussy so much differently than Red. Red ate the whole box; however, the Latino gave focus directly to Aries' clit. She kept her lips tight and wrapped them around Aries' button like a suction cup. She then pulled and pressed Aries' button as if she was giving a blowjob. Aries felt her clit slide in and out of the Latino's wet mouth. The slurping noise sounded with each pull.

Saint watched intensely as he began to get turned on. They were creating a masterpiece. He was halfway erected and walked over to Red. She instantly dropped to her knees and began blowing him. Aries then reached over and began massaging his balls as he got the blowjob. Saint smiled, knowing that Aries was all in. She no longer needed instructions.

By the end of their rendezvous, everyone had orgasmed at least three times. They all lay in the sand, quiet and breathing hard. They were all drained and satisfied. Aries had just experienced the best birthday of her life at the expense of her saint.

***

While Aries and Saint were on the beach, on the other side of town, Crow had Christina's panties around her ankles as he was pounding her out. He was giving her long, strong backstrokes while cupping her chin with his right hand. He pulled her head back with every pump, making her grunt in painful ecstasy with every poke.

"Ugh… ugh… ugh," Christina muttered.

"Cum on dis dick, bitch," Crow said under his breath and he continued to demolish Christina's small frame. Crow took pleasure in knowing that this privileged and spoiled brat was at the end of his pole, getting slutted out. He also got off on the fact that he was banging the plug's daughter. The ultimate no-no. Crow continued to give her a pounding as the sound of his pelvis clapping against her cheeks echoed through the air. Crow was so into what he was doing, he didn't see Chubbs creeping from around the dumpster with his gun in his hand.

He had disappeared for a while, plotting on doing just what he was doing now. He was waiting for the right time to catch Crow slipping and he finally found his opportunity for revenge. Chubbs cocked his gun as he snuck up about twenty feet away from Crow and Christina. Chubbs cocked his gun back and the sound instantly made Crow slide out of Christina and reach down to grab his gun off his belt. He turned, dick out, and began to bust before Chubbs could even let off the first shot. Crow's first bullet caught Chubbs in the leg. Chubbs then returned fire, spitting rounds like a machine gun. He had altered his handgun to shoot like a fully automatic. This alteration was called a "switch." Chubbs let off some rounds and Crow instantly grabbed Christina, using her as a human shield. Bullets entered her abdomen and a single shot went through her neck, killing her instantly.

Crow returned fire and hit Chubbs a few times in the chest, sending him flying onto his back. Crow released Christina's body, letting her limp body fall to the ground. He then walked over to Chubbs as he had blood pouring from his mouth. Chubbs was gasping for air and his body twitched.

Crow stood over him and kicked his gun away from his hand. Crow stood over him and pointed his gun at his head. He saw the life leaving Chubbs and immediately had a sense of gratification. He felt offended that Chubbs would even try him.

"See what yu' get when yu' fuck with a real don dadda. Huh! Yu' see!" Crow yelled with rage in his eyes. Crow stared into Chubbs' eyes and then let off two to his head, sleeping him forever. Crow saw his brains splattered all over the cement and that wasn't enough for him. He then gave him a boot to his head for good measure.

The loud sounds of the afro-beat music drowned out the gunshots, keeping the gunfight private. Crow walked over to Christina and instantly knew that she was dead. Her eyes were wide open and staring into space as blood leaked out of her neck and body.

"Fuck!" Crow said, knowing what was to come. He placed his hands on his head and knew that things were about to get dark. He quickly fled the scene, headed to the trap to try to climb out of the hole that he had just dug for himself.

Chapter Sixteen

WOLVES VS CROWS

Crow was sitting on the porch of the trap. He sliced a mango fruit with his pocketknife. It had been a few days since the murder of Christina and the entire town was on edge. Crow turned down the security job at the resort and tried to remain lowkey on the heels of the recent murder. He was the only one that knew the truth and he had decided to keep his deadly deed a secret to the grave. He knew that he pushed the domino that could potentially turn into a deadly war.

He watched as Saint's pick-up truck pulled onto the block. Saint jumped out and had a stern look on his face. He walked up the steps and didn't acknowledge any of the Crows that were present.

"Let me holla at you," he said, pausing for a second as he walked past Crow. Saint entered the house and Crow followed shortly after. They walked upstairs and Jupe let them in. As soon as the door closed, Saint spoke.

"Yo, what happened?" Saint asked crow.

"Don't know," Crow replied.

"You don't know?"

"Nah. Me no have any information."

"That's funny because I heard your entire crew was inside the club that night," Saint said with skepticism in his tone.

"Yea, me dipped out early. Me had some pussy waiting at de' house," Crow said as he gave a slight smirk.

"Oh yeah?" Saint said as he rubbed his hands together and stared at Crow. He was trying to read Crow's eyes for some sign of deception. He had a feeling in his gut that Crow knew more than he was letting be known. The fact that Chubbs' body was at the scene made him suspicious with him being an ex-member of Crow's crew.

"They say your boy was killed too," Saint added.

"I haven't seen him in months. Me no know what he was doing there."

"Heard you did him dirty a while back," Saint stated.

"Yea, niggas get out of line. Me put straightening on it, yu' know?"

"I got thirty-two missed calls from Diaz. I already know what time he on. This happened on our territory and a spot that we frequent. We need to tell the nigga something or it's going to be up. Feel me?"

Crow nodded his head, agreeing with him. Saint then continued.

"I need some mu'fuckin' answers. Get to the bottom of this shit. ASAP."

"I got yu'," Crow said. His eyes had that look of deceit and Saint's discernment was telling him that Crow was somehow involved or withholding information.

"I'm done with this shit. It's too much shit in the game. After we get this shit figured out, I'm out. I'm done," Saint said, tired of the bullshit.

"What yu' mean?" Crow said as he frowned up.

"You heard me, nigga. I'm out. It's over," Saint confirmed.

Crow instantly began to think about the consequences of Saint leaving the game. That meant outside of Diaz, there was no plug. So, if Diaz cut them off, the game was over. Crow's aspirations of being a drug kingpin were over before they even began. The fact that Diaz was now most likely an opposition, would mean game over.

"That bitch got your head all twisted. She

gotchu' acting pussy," Crow spat, finally speaking his mind.

"Watch yo' fuckin mouth, lil nigga," Saint said as he stepped up to Crow. They were face to face and toe to toe.

"Or what?" Crow said as he clenched his teeth and slid his hand to his gun on his waist.

"What the fuck that mean? Nigga, you ain't the only one with a pistol," Saint said as he smirked and pressed his forehead into Crow's. At that moment, Crow felt a gun to the back of his head. Jupe had slid up on Crow smoothly and placed a snub nose thirty-eight on him.

"Yeah, nigga. You ain't got too much to say now, huh?" Saint said as he reached down and relieved Crow of his gun. Saint had been secretly mentoring and building a relationship with Jupe for the past year. They had grown a bond and Saint strategically kept it a hush-hush for a time like this.

"Damn, Jupe. It's like that?" Crow asked, not believing that his underling had flipped on him.

"Jupe been protecting the money for years and you give him crumbs. See… a nigga like me let my wolves eat. That's the difference between wolves and crows. Wolves run in packs. Crows eat anything and scare off anything that comes near their food. They're selfish. They bitch ass niggas," Saint said with a smug look on his face. Saint stepped back and slid off his shirt. He still had traces of his old physique, despite the boss belly in front of him. He looked at Jupe.

"Hold this, lil man," Saint said as he held out the gun in his direction. . . Jupe took the gun off Crow's head and went to retrieve the gun from Saint. He walked over to the corner and looked on.

Crow put up his fist and they began to circle each other. Crow was the first to swing, catching Saint up in the face with a swift jab. Saint's head snapped back on impact and he quickly focused back on Crow while smiling.

"I eat those, lil nigga," Saint said, bouncing his shoulders, lining up Crow. He swung with a right hook and Crow ducked, just as Saint expected. He already had his left ready to uppercut Crow when he ducked. It caught Crow off guard and he instantly become dizzy from the blow.

"Tighten up, nigga," Saint said.

"Fuck yu'!" yelled Crow.

"Put yo' mu'fucka hands up, nigga," Saint said as he held up his fist.

He decided to give Crow a fair one. He was about to teach him a lesson about respect. It was time to finally discipline Crow. Saint swung on Crow and although Crow blocked it; the power still knocked him to his knees. Saint then gave Crow a swift kick to the head, sending him flying on his back. Saint knew he had about thirty more seconds before he got winded. He wasn't a spring chicken anymore and that old nigga breathing began to creep in. So, Saint went in for the finisher. He straddled Crow and began to choke him out. He wrapped both of his hands around Crow's neck and squeezed him as hard as he could. Veins began to form in Crow's forehead as the brute strength of Saint was stopping his air circulation. Crow tried to pry his hands away, but Saint was too strong.

"Don't you ever disrespect me. I'll kill you, mu'fucka," Saint said as he disciplined him. He watched as Crow struggled and his eyes started to roll behind his head. Crow's body was beginning to go limp and that's when Saint released him. Crow instantly gasped for air and held his neck. Saint stood up and look down on Crow in disgust.

"Let's go, Jupe," Saint said as he stepped over Crow as he squirmed on the ground, still struggling to catch his breath. Saint and Jupe left Crow there in the moneyless room. Saint had already cleared the trap and he was shutting down shop for good. He was done with the game. But first, he had to clear the air with Diaz.

***

Aries flipped the closed sign on the restaurant and took a deep breath. She had a long day at the restaurant and was glad her day was over. She looked down at her watch and then put her hands on her hips. She hadn't gotten her delivery of money from Diaz and she found it odd. Since they had been doing business, he had never been late. Every first of the month, at the same time, she would get a ring at the doorbell and then a box on the porch always full of money. She had no idea of the recent death of Christina; however, she would soon find out.

Trey came in and without saying anything, headed up the stairs.

"Aye... aye! Whoa. Yu' not gon to speak to yu' mama?" Aries said with her arms crossed, walking towards the staircase. Aries frowned as she smelled a weed aroma trailing Trey. He stopped at the bottom of the stairs and looked down, avoiding eye contact.

"Hello," Trey said dryly with annoyance in his tone. Aries snapped her head back and frowned.

"What's been going on with yu'? Yu' smoking? Talking crazy to me? What happened to me baby boy, eh?" Aries asked in confusion.

"It's nothing, Mom. I'm just doing me."

"Doing yu'?" Aries asked as she stepped to Trey.

She could see that his eyes were red and she felt a sense of disappointment. Not because he was smoking, but the fact that Trey didn't tell her. They had a close bond and they never hid things from one another. For the first time, Aries felt a disconnect.

"This ain't yu', Trey," Aries said, shaking her head in disappointment.

"You're right. I'm a softy… remember," Trey said before he turned and left Aries standing there in shame. She knew that he had overheard her conversation with Miamor.

"Damn," Aries said under her breath. She felt horrible knowing that she hurt her boy's feelings. She wanted to go upstairs and make things right, but she wanted to give him time to cool off.

Chapter Seventeen

PAIN TRICKLES

Diaz looked down at the body of his precious daughter as she laid on the coroner's table. His eyes were filled with tears and his heart was heavy.

"My dear Christina. I love you so much sweetheart," he whispered just before he bent down and kissed her cold forehead. He had felt the greatest pain a father could feel and that was losing a child. Also, in the manner that it happened only added to his despair. He stared at her and she wasn't even recognizable. Her head was swollen and her lips were purple. He stepped back and took a deep breath as he looked at the coroner and nodded his head. The coroner swiftly stepped to the table and pulled the sheet over her head, not wanting Diaz to suffer any longer. Diaz turned around and exited the room. His two henchmen were waiting for him and followed him towards the building's exit.

Diaz's sad face quickly turned into one of anger. As they exited the building, Diaz was turning to violence if he didn't get answers to his questions about his precious daughter. He didn't care about anything or anybody anymore. At that point, all that he saw was red. Just as he stepped off the front stairs of the coroner's office, his sprinter was waiting on the curb with the door open so that Diaz could slide right in.

Before he reached the car, Crow came from the side of the building with his hands up, showing that he was no threat.

"Diaz! Let me talk to yu'. Just need a few minutes!" Crow yelled as he walked towards Diaz and his crew comprehensively. Immediately, Diaz's henchmen pulled out their guns, pointing them, and ready to blow Crow's head off. It made Crow stop in his tracks. His hands remained in the air, and he never took his focus off Diaz.

"Please… give me just a minute. Me know what happened to yu' daughter," Crow said.

"What the fuck did you just say?" Diaz asked as he frowned and began to walk towards Crow. One of his henchmen quickly grabbed the back of Crow's neck, while placing his gun to Crow's temple. Crow felt the cold steel digging into his skin and the goon held his head down so that he was now looking at the ground as he was being handled aggressively.

"Me said... me know what happened to yu' daughter," Crow repeated, choosing his words carefully. Diaz looked at his goon and threw his head in the direction of his truck. Almost immediately the goon hurried Crow to the sprinter and violently threw him in the backseat. Diaz slid in next to him and the goons closed the doors, leaving them in the backseat to talk.

"You need to talk and talk quick," Diaz said with tears in his eyes and fire in his chest.

"Me found out some shit that me wanted to tell yu'," Crow stated.

"Talk!" Diaz screamed, raising his voice to the highest octave possible. He had a crazed look in his eyes and his body trembled vigorously.

"It was Saint. He called de' hit for me' little nigga Chubbs."

Diaz grabbed Crow by the collar and pulled him close.

"What the fuck did you say?" Diaz asked.

"Saint. He called de' hit and Christina got hit in de' crossfire. He told me to keep it a secret," Crow lied, trying to kill two birds with one stone. He wanted to get in good graces with Diaz and get Saint knocked off. He thought about this plan in detail and figured out that it was a brilliant idea.

"So... Saint made the call?" Diaz asked, wanting him to be crystal clear.

"Yes. He called it," Crow said with confidence. Diaz just stared at Crow, trying to sense any type of dishonesty.

"He hasn't returned my call," Diaz said to himself as he looked away as if he was in deep thought.

"That's because he's laying low," Crow replied.

"I want blood. I want blood and I want it now. Does he have kids?" Diaz asked the sinister thought began to creep into his thoughts.

"No... no kids," Crow said. He knew Diaz was ready to go to the limit for retribution after hearing his question. "But he love that bitch," Crow added.

"Aries?" Diaz asked.

"Yep."

"I want her dead. I want her son dead. I want someone to feel the pain that I'm feeling. The thing about pain is that it's contagious. It's a cancer. If it gets in someone close to you, it eventually trickles to you."

"Her son. Trey?" Crow asked in confusion.

"That's right."

"He's a kid," Crow said, knowing that Diaz was taking it too far.

Diaz grabbed Crow by his shirt and pulled him close. His jaws were clenched and he had a death stare.

"I don't give a shit! I want him dead! I want them to feel this pain that I'm feeling before I gut them like fuckin' fishes. Both of them!" Diaz yelled as he released Crow and pushed him, making him fly back into his seat. Diaz took a few deep breaths and fixed his own shirt as he tried to regain his composure.

"Do me get his spot if me make this happen?" Crow asked.

Diaz simply nodded his head, signaling the answer that Crow had been waiting for his entire criminal career. The gesture made Crow's dick hard and greed formed in his soul. He was obsessed. He wanted the power. He wanted to be the Top Shootah.

***

"Yu' want to be a Crow, right? This is yu' chance," Crow said as he sat at the table of his small home. Jalen was across from him with his head down. He was conflicted. He felt guilt for what he was contemplating doing. Crow looked at his little brother intensely. He saw the hesitation in his eyes. Crow slammed his fist on the table, making Jalen jump in fear as he looked at Crow.

"Why are you doing this man? He's a square," Jalen said, looking like he was about to cry.

"It came from the top. Saint called the play," Crow said, knowing that it would hold more weight coming from the head honcho.

"If I do it, I'll be down with the crew for real?" Jalen asked. He had been wanting to be a part of his brother's team all his life and Crow never showed any desire in letting him do so.

"Me swear on our mudda," Crow confirmed.

"Okay, I'll do it."

It was a great night. Jalen and Trey were on the sands of the shore. A group of young adults circled around a gigantic bonfire. The Crows were amongst the gathering, partying, and having a good time. Beer and ganja were flowing. Jalen rocked a freshly done M.O.C tattoo on the side of his neck. It was just after midnight and the moonlight bounced off the ocean. Trey snuck out the house, knowing that his mother wouldn't approve of him being out that late.

"Yo, you feeling good tonight?" Jalen asked Trey as he held out the bottle neck towards Trey.

Trey extended his as well as they clinked the beers.

"Yea, this is pretty cool," Trey said, enjoying the freedom of being out in the wee hours of the night, something he never did. However, he was upset with his mother and it pushed him to be rebellious.

"Check me out, my boy!" Jalen said as he turned to the side and showed the tattoo on his neck that was shiny and covered in balm to keep it disinfected.

"Nice! He finally let you in?" Trey asked, smiling from ear to ear, genuinely happy for his friend.

"I'm fuckin' with da gangsters now. All the way plugged in," Jalen said as he chuckled and held out his hand in celebration with his friend.

"Let's get it," Trey said genuinely excited.

Jalen felt guilty for even contemplating doing something to Trey. The conversation he had with Crow was heavy on his heart.

"You know what... you my nigga. I appreciate you being my homie. You a' great friend," Jalen said as grabbed both of his shoulders and looked in his eyes with a big smile.

"We boys for life," Trey said as he reached out his hand and they locked up and then briefly hugged. After a quick embrace, Jalen playfully pushed Trey off him and laughed.

"Man, these Coronas got you in your feelings. Fuck you, man," Jalen said jokingly.

"Forget you," Trey replied while smiling.

"Listen, Sparkle and her girls trying to get it in back at the trap," Jalen stated.

"I don't know. I snuck out and don't wanna stay out too late. She wake up early and I don't wanna get caught up."

"Man, come on. We just going to mess around with them and we out."

"I don't know, bro," Trey answered, while slowly shaking his head, not wanting to press his luck.

"It's a big day for me. I decided to stand on loyalty. More than you know…"

"What are you talking about?" Trey asked, not understanding what Jalen was getting at.

"Never mind. Just know that I got your back. Look man, is we going to get this pussy or what? I'm trying to celebrate tonight," Jalen said as he pointed at his neck tattoo.

"Alright man. Not for long though. Mess with them for a while… then we out."

"Bet. We out," Jalen said as he threw his arm around Trey's neck and downed the rest of his beer.

***

"Welcome home, bitch."

"Thanks, Betty," Miamor replied. Aries could hear the joy in her voice. Aries sat on her balcony smoking a joint as she enjoyed the rare full moon. It was just after midnight. The cool breeze and mist in the air relaxed Aries as she sucked the smoke into her lungs. She held her cell phone to her ear with her free hand and her feet were kicked up, resting on the ledge.

"Why are you still up?" Miamor asked.

"Just waiting for Trey to bring his ass home. He snuck his lil' ass out and thought me didn't know. Me just let him go and didn't say shit. Give him a little freedom, yu' know?"

"I feel you, girl. Them children a mu'fucka ain't they? They don't get that we were young at one point. Ain't nothing they can do that we ain't saw or done. Especially us. We stayed on some bullshit," Miamor said.

"Yeah, we were wild. Anyways, how does it feel to be out? Me know yu' glad to be home, eh?"

"I'm blessed. I just want to catch up on lost time. CJ around this bitch running wild. He's just like his daddy and uncles used be. Wild than a mu'fucka. I gotta lot of catching up to do. I'mma get him on the right track," Miamor explained.

"Yu' know how that go. De' more you try to pull

him away, de' more he's going to gravitate to it. De' streets is in him. It's in his blood."

"You gotta point. I'll figure it out. I just have to get back in tune with everything. I been gone for a while."

"After me figure shit out, I'mma have to come see yu'."

"Nah, you stay yo' ass right where you at. I'mma come see you. I just gotta keep this PO off my ass. Once I get settled and get this PO off my ass, I'mma come see ya'll. I miss you like crazy."

"Me miss you too, Mia," Aries replied.

"Did you make the appointment?" Miamor asked.

"Yea, I did. I keep going back and forth. I just don't know... I just don't know," Aries said, not being sure about her decision to get an abortion. She had yet to tell Saint, knowing that he would want to keep it. But Aries knew that a child with a man was a permanent bond with another person. The way her life was set up, she didn't have the luxury of stability. At any moment, she was prepared to pick up and leave any place at any time.

"Do you love him?" Miamor asked.

"What love have to do with it?

***

Saint sat at the table looking at Crow. Saint gripped his gun under the table, ready for anything Crow had under his sleeve. He was trying to read him. Crow had called him and requested a sit down. Crow had tears in his eyes and a busted lip as he pleaded with his big homie.

"Look. Me fucked up. Yu' been nothin' but good to me. After me moms and poppa die, yu' took me under yu' wing. The thirst for power consumed me," Crow pleaded.

Saint remained quiet and watched as the tears began to fall on Crow's face. Saint understood that Crow wasn't wrapped too tight and this kept him skeptical.

"I'm sorry, Saint," Crow said as the tears began to flow. The sadness in his eyes were sincere and the realization that he needed Saint sunk in. Saint's jaws were clenched tightly and he side-eyed his former protégé. Crow stood and Saint quickly did the same with his gun in hand.

"Please forgive me," Crow begged as he slowly approached Saint, sobbing like a baby.

He reached out his hands and slowly approached Saint. Crow hugged him and then broke down in his arms. Saint felt Crow's body trembling as he huffed and puffed, begging for forgiveness. Crow buried his head into Saint's chest, wetting up his shirt with his waterfall. Saint was confused and didn't know if he should console him or blow his head off. That's when Saint realized that Crow was young and didn't know how to move correctly. He wondered if was it his own fault for not giving him the proper guidance.

As Saint was thinking about all of this, Crow was slowly reaching down into his waist to pull out the small caliber gun. He gripped it and raised it up, giving Saint two shots to the chest. Saint's eyes bucked as he lost his breath, making him drop his gun. He gripped his chest and fell onto the ground. Crow looked down at him and the fake tears instantly stopped as a smirk formed on his face. He stood over him with a sinister gaze. He pointed his gun at Saint's head, remembering how Saint had beaten him up. To Crow, revenge never felt so good.

He was about to squeeze again, but the sounds of feet running down the stairs made him pause. Knowing Saint, he guessed that he had someone guarding him in the house. Crow swiftly ran out the back door, feeling good about what he had just done. His plan was coming together just as he had calculated.

***

Aries sat in the corner of Jimmy's at 2 a.m. She needed to get fresh air and clear her mind. It felt like the weight of so many things were on her all at once. The upcoming abortion, the feds on her heels, and the disconnect with Trey; it all seemed to be too much. Aries took a deep pull of the weed and looked around the nearly empty bar. It was a weekday so the traffic was minimum just like Aries liked it. She saw Red from across the floor and gave her a grin. Red winked back. As Red, wiped off the bar top; she couldn't stop smiling at Aries. Red wiped her hands dry and walked around the counter headed in the direction of Aries.

As she made over to Aries, a young lady burst through the door into the bar. Aries instantly noticed her. It was one of the waitresses that she had seen around the bar. She hurried up to Red and said something to her. Red instantly got a worried look and put her hand over her mouth. Aries watched as it was obvious that Red had gotten bad news. Red immediately looked over to Aries with tears in her eyes. Aries frowned and wondered what was wrong with her. Red hurried to Aries.

"What's wrong?" Aries asked as she sat up in her chair.

"Oh, my God. Oh, my God..." Red said as sadness was all over her face.

"What? What happened?" Aries asked, trying to figure out what Red was trying to say.

"They killed him," Red said as the tears finally fell.

Aries dropped her head, knowing what the streets sometimes did. She didn't want to believe that Saint was gone. She felt the tears forming in her eyes and the lump forming in her throat.

"Oh no... they killed Saint," Aries said, not wanting to hear the answer. She instantly knew that Diaz or Crow had something to do with it.

"No... they found Trey. They shot him in the head. I'm so sorry, Aries," Red admitted as the sadness seemed to fill the room.

"What did yu' say?" Aries asked as she stood up and hoped to God that she had just misheard.

"They found him in a house. Oh my God... Aries they found him."

"No, no, no, no, no..." Aries fell to her knees as she felt lightheaded and her knees got weak. Her worst nightmare had come true. The streets had claimed her son. Her naïve son was gone.

One Hour Earlier

"Where everybody at? They said they would meet us here," Jalen said as he walked in the house and flicked on the light. Trey followed him in and looked around in confusion.

"What up, bro? Thought you said Sparkle and dem' was coming."

"Go look in back room and see if they back there," Jalen said as he threw his head in the direction of the back of the house.

"Huh?" Trey said in confusion as he looked towards the back and noticed that the lights were off.

"Nobody is back there, bro. What are you talking about?" Trey said while smiling.

"Trust me. Check it out," Jalen assured with a friendly face.

"Okay, cool."

Trey headed to the back and Jalen followed closely behind. Trey reached the room and turned on the lights. It was an empty room. Only thing that was in the room was the plastic that lined the floor. Trey was confused as he looked around.

"Nothing is back here. What's..." Trey stopped talking mid-sentence when he turned around. He saw that Jalen had a black Glock nine pointed to his head.

"Jalen! What you doing, bro?" Trey asked as he put his hands up.

"Sorry. I have to do this," Jalen said as his hand trembled as he held the gun.

"Stop playing with that thing. That's dangerous. Quit messing around," Trey said, not understanding what was going on.

"Just close your eyes, man. I promise it won't hurt," Jalen said as the shame took over his body.

"What you mean, man? Why are you pointing a gun at me? I thought we were boys, man?" Trey said as his voice began to tremble.

"Just close your fuckin' eyes, Trey! Please."

Trey's bottom lips began to quiver and his heart was beating so hard; he felt like a baboon was trying to escape from his chest. Trey began to sob.

"Jalen. Please stop playing. I'm scared, man. This is freaking me out, bro," Trey said as he began to sob uncontrollably. All his limbs were shaking and the harsh reality began to set in when he saw the seriousness in Jalen's eyes.

"We're best friends, man. You the best friend I ever had, man. Why are you…"

BOOM!

Jalen sent a slug straight through Trey's forehead and watched his body drop instantly. Jalen was so nervous that he dropped the gun after the shot. His adrenaline pumped and he couldn't stop his hands from shaking. He looked down at Trey and his body began to twitch wildly. Jalen was frozen in fear and his mind began to race. Eventually, he stopped as his eyes stared into space and his body went limp. Trey had taken his last breath at the hands of his closest comrade. He felt sad, but the thought of him being a Crow ruled all. He had just experienced his rite of passage.

***

Saint slowly sat up while holding his chest. His chest ached from the gunshot that Crow had sent at him. Saint watched as Crow escaped out of the back and Jupe came from upstairs with his gun drawn.

"Big homie! You good?" Jupe asked as he looked around, looking for Crow.

"Yeah, I'm good," Saint replied as he ripped open his linen shirt, exposing his bulletproof vest. Jupe saw the two holes that were smoking out of the Teflon.

"My bad," Jupe said, feeling bad about not getting downstairs in time.

"You are good. You did exactly what you supposed to do. Protect Lovey. All good."

Jupe helped Saint up and by the look on his face, Jupe knew the war was on.

Chapter Eighteen

EMOTIONLESS

Aries was draped in all back with an oversized, stylish top hat, sheer draped down over her face. Aries watched as the graveyard workers tossed dirt on the casket of her son. She watched emotionless, still not believing what had become her life. Her baby was gone. She held a secret service and only a few were there. Miamor and CJ were on each side of her. Miamor had tears in her eyes as she rubbed her friend's back, trying to console her. However, Aries had cried non-stop for the past week. She had no more tears to give. She was ready for blood.

"Auntie, I think we should leave. You shouldn't watch this part," CJ said as he placed his hand on her shoulder. Aries stared down into the hole, watching the dirt blanket her son. Aries wasn't blinking or mobbing. It was like she wasn't even there. She was detached from reality.

Miamor wanted to say something to her sister, but she couldn't find the words. She knew that she just had to be there for her. She wasn't even legally cleared to be in the Caribbeans, but she didn't care. She had to come and help her sister through the hard time.

"Come on. Let's go," CJ suggested.

Aries took a few steps towards the edge of the hole and dropped a rose down and closed her eyes. A single tear dropped and she quickly wiped it away. She promised it would be her last tear until after she killed whoever did this to her son. She turned and walked away, not wanting to see anymore. Aries was broken and everything that was good about her was six feet deep.

Miamor and CJ followed close behind as the black SUV waited for them at the graveyard's path. CJ looked in the direction of the two sedans that were a few feet behind them. CJ nodded his head at them, signaling them to follow him. He had brought seven goons from Miami and they were all on go. They were ready to tear up the island and anyone in it, at CJ's request. He opened the door for his mom and aunt and got in the driver's seat. He pulled off with his killers trailing. Miamor felt the pain of her best friend and knew it was nothing that she could say to provide comfort. So, she held her hand and without saying a word, let her know that she was there for her. Miamor looked at Aries, but she couldn't see her. It was as if she wasn't there. Aries' mind was not present. She was numb.

"Auntie, I know you might not want to hear this…" CJ said as he steered the truck out of the cemetery.

"I want to know everything," Aries interrupted.

"We found out who pulled the trigger," CJ said. Miamor felt Aries' hand tense up and the rage was burning from within. However, her face was without reaction.

"Take me to 'em," Aries said simply. CJ nodded his head and turned out the cemetery.

Aries' phone rang, which broke up the monotony. Aries grabbed her phone from her purse and looked at it. The name "Saint Von" was on the screen and she immediately sent him to voicemail. She didn't want to talk to anyone that had anything to do with the island that claimed her son. Aries had cut everyone off, including Saint. Fuck pity… Aries wanted blood. The island had no idea that they had awakened a monster. Aries and Miamor were just different. They had been through so many wars and tribulations.

***

Saint looked down at his phone and shook his head. He had been trying to contact Aries for over a week and he got nothing. He heard about what happened to Trey and immediately felt heartbroken for his lady. The fact that she cut off communication had him boggled. He had minimum information on what was the reason for the death of her son. The only thing that he knew was that Trey was last seen with Jalen. Saint couldn't help but think this was directly from his beef with Crow.

Maybe Crow wanted to hurt me... so in return, he hurt Aries. Trey was a casualty of war. Everything is so fucked up, Saint thought as he put away his phone.

He was on his way to the trap to see if he could catch Crow, Jalen, or anybody for that matter. Everyone was laying low and the trap had been shut down. No Crows showed their faces and Crow was nowhere in sight. The block was deserted and everything was in question. Saint pulled onto the block and what he saw totally blew his mind. In all his years, he had never witnessed anything even close to what he was currently seeing. It was as if he was driving down the corridors of hell.

***

CJ pulled into a big, vacant lot that sat behind Diaz's manufacturing building. No one had been there since Christina was murdered so it seemed like a ghost town. CJ's goons pulled up as well. CJ put the car in park and jumped out. He quickly opened the door for his mother and aunt. Aries looked confused as she looked around, not sure exactly why they were there.

"What's up wit' dis?" Aries asked as her face frowned.

"I got something to show you," CJ said as he watched the two of them step out. He then closed the door and walked over to one of the cars that the goons were in. He walked over to the trunk and waved them over.

"After shaking shit up, we found out some info. Lil 'cuz was with his boy, Jalen, the night he got murdered," CJ said carefully, trying not to be harsh in his delivery of the news. Aries closed her eyes and it was bittersweet. It was good to get any news about what happened; however, the words "murdered" and "Trey" were like sharp daggers to her heart.

"We found everybody we needed to find, auntie. The lil' nigga, Jalen, had a tattoo on his neck, pointing us in the direction we needed to go. The Crows, right?" CJ asked calmly. Aries nodded her head in confirmation. That's when CJ popped the trunk.

A man was bound and gagged. He was hogtied and squirming like a fish, trying to release himself from the bondage. It was Crow in the trunk. His face was bloody and his eyes were swollen shut from the beating he had been getting for the past twelve hours.

"We wanted you to hear what he told us. That's the only reason, he ain't dead," CJ said. He reached to his waist and grabbed his pistol. He then pointed it at Crow's head. With his free hand, he pulled down the rag that was stuffed down his throat. Aries crossed her arms and watched calmly. Her facial expression still was blank... nothing.

"I'm going to ask you this once and only once. Who killed Trey?" CJ asked.

"Me don't know," Crow said under his breath, trying to keep what dignity that he had left. CJ reached his hand back so he could pistol whip him, but Aries reached and grabbed his arm. Aries then grabbed the gun from CJ and swung it directly at Crow.

"Who killed me boy, eh?" Aries asked tranquilly.

"I told you! Me don't know!" Crow yelled. Aries wasn't convinced so she slid the gun from Crow's head and now it was pointed at his crotch.

"I'm going to count to three. If me don't get answer... yu' balls getting blew off. One..."

Bang!

Aries fired a shot, causing a small spark followed by a loud sound of a gunshot. Crow yelled in excruciating pain.

"Aghhh!!"

"Okay! Okay!" Crow yelled as his crotch burned like hell. His mind was racing and he knew that a gunshot to his head was next if he didn't give some sort of information. He knew that he killed Saint, so he decided to blame it on a dead man.

"Saint! Saint made de' call!" Crow yelled.

"What?" Aries asked, not understanding.

"Saint! Diaz told him that if he didn't kill Trey that he would kill him. He wanted him to feel de' same pain he felt. He knew that Saint loved yu'. So he decided to hurt yu' so Saint would have to pick up de' pieces."

"What de' fuck are yu' talking bout?" Aries asked, trying to take in all that Crow had just alleged.

"Saint called de' hit on Chubbs and Diaz's daughter got hit in de' crossfire," Crow lied. Aries didn't want to hear anymore. She just looked at Crow in disgust and shook her head. She handed the gun back to CJ.

"Me want his head cut off. Slowly," Aries demanded. Miamor remained silent and knew that the old Aries was back.

"Say less, auntie," CJ said as he closed the trunk and looked over to his goons, giving them the head nod to follow the orders of Aries.

"One more thing," Miamor said as she placed her hand on Aries' shoulder.

"What?" Aries asked as she tried her best to not drop a tear. Her eyes were filled with tears and at any second, one could fall.

"Come on," Miamor said as she walked back to the truck. Her, CJ, and Aries got in and pulled off.

CJ drove directly to the trap; the block where all the Crows hustled on. Aries was unsure why they were there, but she would soon find out. As they slowly made their way down the street, Miamor pointed up and ahead out of the front window, wanting Aries to look. Aries followed Miamor's finger and saw a body lynched from each light down the entire block. She saw Jalen with a noose around his neck. His M.O.C tattoo showed clearly as his lifeless body swayed. Six members of the Crows were hanging like fruit from a tree; all dead and swinging in the air. CJ made sure he drove slowly, so Aries could take in what they had done— Cartel style.

As they crept down the block, Aries saw Saint's truck coming towards them. Aries was in a tinted truck, so he didn't notice them. She watched as looked in awe at the gory scene.

"That's homeboy, right?" CJ asked, having already did his homework on everyone. CJ pulled out his gun and placed it on his lap.

"Yeah, that's him. But don't do anything now," Aries said as she tapped the seat, making sure CJ listened to her.

"Me want him and anyone in de' house murdered. Me want heads!"

"Understood," CJ said as he looked back at his auntie and then his mom. Miamor glanced at Aries as they pulled off the block.

"Maybe, you need to reschedule that little thing? Today was a lot," Miamor said, suggesting that Aries should cancel the abortion procedure that she had arranged. Aries quickly shook her head no, mentally preparing herself for what was about to go down.

"No, I gotta get dis man's baby out of me."

***

The smell of burnt breakfast sausage and the fire alarm sounded throughout the air, waking

294

Saint from his peaceful slumber. He instantly sat up and took a deep breath as he wiped the cold from his eyes. He stretched his hands above his head and let out a toe-curling yawn. He quickly went to the French doors that led to the ocean. He smiled and shook his head, knowing that his Lovey had probably gotten too caught up in her morning talk shows and burnt breakfast.

Saint rubbed his slightly protruding belly that sat just above his beltline. Saint wasn't fat by any means, but the extra belly came from years of good eating and living the good life. His shoulders and arms were intact; the stomach in front of him showed his comfortable lifestyle. He smiled as he ran his tongue over his top row of teeth. They were perfect and white... opposite the bottom row. Pure gold slugs were across his bottom row, giving a rugged look. Although Saint was very articulate, intelligent, and stoic; his gold slugs were a pure indication of what he was. His full, neatly trimmed beard was perfectly symmetrical around his lips, and he had a beautiful smile. Some would call him a monster, but the ones that truly knew him called him a saint. The irony.

"Lovey! You left the stove on again!" Saint yelled as he looked back, so his grandmother could hear him from where he was in the back bedroom.

Saint paused and waited for her response. The only thing he heard was the loud sounds of Wendy Williams coming from the television. He smiled and shook his head, knowing that she was hard of hearing and always would blast the television, but she usually waited until he was up before her shenanigans started.

"Alright, Lovey... here I come," Saint said to himself as he smiled and shook his head.

He loved living with his grandma in her home country. It had been her dream to come back to the islands and live out the remainder of her life. So, about a year before, Saint had purchased her an immaculate villa right off the ocean. He relocated her there for good. It was something that Saint needed as well. He needed an escape from his former life in the States. He had done many things on the wrong side of the law and was fortunate enough to avoid jail time or, even worse, death. Lovey would thank him every morning for making her dreams come true, but Saint was even more thankful. He loved that he could see his only living relative every single day, and just like in old times, she would make him breakfast every morning and even made his bed for him at night.

Although Saint was well off and could afford to housekeep, it meant more to him to make his grandmother feel needed. They were two peas in a pod, and Saint was happier than he'd been in a while. His grandmother was his best friend. His quality of life had elevated since they both moved to the island.

Saint quickly ran water over his face and threw on a t-shirt before heading into the kitchen area, which sat in the middle of the luxury villa. Lovey always wanted a spacious kitchen, and Saint ensured she had more. She had more than enough room to cook anytime she wanted. Saint rubbed his stomach and knew that Lovey was part of why he was holding some of that gut.

"What you got burning in here, girl?" Saint playfully said as he walked onto the marble floors that opened to the kitchen area. Saint walked in smiling, and the first thing he saw was smoke coming from the stove area.

"Oh shit," he whispered as he hurried over to the stove.

The smoke detector was still beeping and made things more chaotic. Also, the sound of the television being to the max was distracting. As Saint approached the stove, he quickly turned the burner off. There were six sausage links in the skillet, burned to a crisp. He looked over to the stove and saw burnt biscuits inside as well.

"Grandma!" Saint yelled, only using that name when he was in trouble or something was wrong. "Girl, you un' forgot about everything! Almost burned the house down," Saint said while laughing to himself, grabbing the skillet, and placing it over the sink.

He turned on the water to cool the skillet, causing a gush of steam to rise into the air. Everything seemed so hectic because of all the noises, not to mention the nerve racking alarm. Saint hurried over to the kitchen drawer to grab a dish towel to fan the alarm. Saint felt something wet on the floor, and he quickly raised his foot while looking down. It was a red liquid.

"What the fuck?" Saint whispered as he squinted his eyes.

He then noticed that it was coming from somewhere. His eyes followed the path of the thick, maroon color liquid and everything froze when he saw the source of the blood. It was Lovey. In a matter of a second, time froze. He didn't hear the loudness of the television anymore. He didn't hear the irritating sound of the smoke detector nor the sound of the sizzling from the sausages. The only sense that was working was his sight. He had become entirely numb. He looked down at her body, which had on a morning gown and a cooking apron. As his eyes slowly traveled up her body, he saw the unthinkable. Her head was severed from her body. It was completely gone. Guts and body pieces he'd never seen before were spilling from her neck, where her head used to be.

"No... no... no, Grandma," Saint said as he dropped to his knees, trying to put the contents spilling out of her neck back into the corpse. He was in shock; his mind didn't know what to do. His hands shook vigorously, and his eyes bucked as he examined her bloody body. Saint's hands fidgeted nervously around what used to be the woman he held closest to his heart. He sat on his knees and felt like he was in the middle of a nightmare. He instantly stood up and looked around. He yelled for Jupe; his personal shooter that always protected his home while he was asleep. He would station himself on the front porch and walk around the house every night.

"Jupe!!! Jupe!!!" Saint yelled as he looked around feverishly, searching for his personal bodyguard. It wasn't until he stepped out of the kitchen and partially into the living room that he saw Jupe. His body was lying there, lifeless... also decapitated. Jupe's head was missing from his body. Saint's stomach dropped at the gruesome sight . Saint was stuck.

As he looked closer, he noticed that the eyes of Lovey and Jupe were looking at him. Their two heads were lined up inside Lovey's China cabinet on top of two dish plates. One head on each platter. The heads were on display as if it was a twisted art exhibit. Saint stiffened and blinked his bloodshot red eyes, not believing what he saw was real. However, it was true. This was his reality. This wasn't a dream by any stretch of the imagination. It was karma….

***

Aries heard a knock on the door and quickly grabbed her gun. CJ gripped his as well, following his aunt's lead. Aries crept to the door, stood on her tiptoes, and looked in through the peephole.

"Oh, we're good," Aries said as she looked back at CJ to relax him. She opened the door and smiled.

"Oh me God. Where have you been, girl?" Aries smiled and opened her arms. Flower, wild hair and all, was standing in front of her. Aries hugged her tightly and rocked back and forth. She missed Flower so much and she had never been more excited to see her. She let Flower in and quickly hid her bloody hands. Aries smiled. She noticed the skeptic and confusion on Miamor and CJ's faces. They were wondering why she would let the young lady in while they were in the aftermath of the murders.

"Don't worry, she doesn't understand," Aries assured them as she guided Flower into the kitchen to join them.

"Sit down, baby, let me make yu' something to eat," Aries said as she pulled the chair out for Flower. She then looked at Miamor and began to speak.

"Me hope it kills him when he sees his grand mudda's head cut off. Fuck em! After he buries her... I'mma send 'em right behind her."

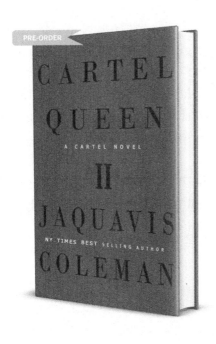

CARTEL QUEEN 2 COMING FALL 2023

Pre-order and use code "QUEEN2" for 30% off
At www.colemanbooks.com

2nd Edition

Made in United States
Orlando, FL
08 March 2025

59260446R00177